GEORGIANA'S TWINKLE

SOMETIMES, SOMEONE MAKES A HEART TWINKLE

MANSI SARAF

Made with ♥ on the Notion Press Platform
www.notionpress.com

*To the little girl who once dreamed of
becoming a writer.
Now, here we are.
Yay, little girl — Mansi.*

Contents

Contents

Preface

I have seen so many love stories around us —
some that complete like magic,
some that remain incomplete, leaving behind a special note,
and some that end with a really painful goodbye.

But... we should never lose hope.
We should never lose the courage to retry,
or the power to give love — not only to our loved ones but
to everyone around us.

Caring for someone feels like a gentle hand placed
softly on our head — bringing comfort, strength, warmth,
and the assurance of having someone to whom we really
matter, and who really matters to us.

As the audacity of human care — like the brush of lips
on a soft cheek.

Maybe... miracles happen when we least expect them.

— Mansi

Acknowledgements

First and foremost, I thank the little girl within me who always dreamt of becoming a writer when she grew up.
And see the irony — now she is at an age where she never thought she would actually do so!

I am forever grateful to *Mr. Shelindra Saraf [my dad] and Dr. Neelam Saraf [my mum]*, who were always excited to hear where my story had reached.

To my sisters, *Manvi Saraf and Aashika Jain*, who always thought about the next moments of my characters and said, "When will the perfect moment come?"

To my friend, *Suryansh Singh*, who just said yes to my crazy idea of writing this kind of story, and laughed saying, "Haha, how crazy, Mansi!"

I would also like to thank every reader who chooses to walk into the city of Georgiana to see its magic in the hearts of people — your presence makes every word twinkle a little brighter.

And lastly, a heartfelt thank you to the little moments of hope, love, emotions, and dreams that inspired this story.

— Mansi

Note On Narrative Style

In Georgiana's Twinkle, the chapters featuring Rinzee are written in the first person, offering a deeper, more personal view of her thoughts and emotions. The rest of the story is told from the third-person perspective, providing insight into the lives of the other characters. This choice was made to create a contrast between Rinzee's inner world and the perspectives of those around her.

CHAPTER ONE

A New Beginning

Today, I'm very excited, yet there's a feeling of leaving my special ones behind. [grinning] We're moving to **Georgiana** – a magical city full of beaches and heavy snowfall. I saw snowfall at the beach when I was fifteen.

Oh, I forgot to introduce myself! I'm **Rinzee Woodrock** –*kind-hearted, sweet, and (as they say) blessed with a cute voice.* My family, the **Woodrocks**, has a long history in our previous city, **Rinny**, which means 'shine'.

Obviously, Rinny would have a special place in my heart, as there I found my friends—**Tera** and **Kam**. Tera and Kam have been with me since I was in class five. They have helped me so much.

But... but... but... [smirking] I don't think they remember me.

Aann....! My mum...!

My mum, Isabelle Woodrock, an open-minded lady, sweet, caring, hmm... caring! She's so kind and caring for their kids, oh... no... no... no... she calls us – kiddos. I think that suits her personality. [grinning and staring at my mum.]

Oh, we reached Georgiana!

Isabelle Woodrock (Rinzee's mother) – Rinzee, see, it's your dream city! This city is all about magic in the air. I think our life will be filled with happy vibes, with people who have magic within them.

Rinzee, don't be sad about leaving things behind. We have to go with the flow of life and should give a chance to the future as well. Sometimes, we don't see the things that are good and joyful for us, but we have to enjoy both the bad and good experiences in life. And it's your dream city, so enjoy everything that nature and life give you.

[I nodded slowly.] – Mum, hmm, I'll enjoy every moment that this beautiful nature gives me.

Mum, as you already know, I have loved this city since my childhood. Oh, this city! When I came here for the first time, I was like, Georgiana?

What a pretty name!

I fell in love with the name of this city too.

Tera and Kam are also very happy and excited for me, knowing that I am moving to this beautiful city. I wish they could be with us in this place—it feels like heaven when snowfall blankets the beach. Even in summer, the beach feels like home.

Aahh! So excited!

(Phone rings.)

Hello, Tera! *[I smirk]* Oh... so she actually called me!

Tera – Hey Rinzee, have you reached?

Almost, Tera. I'm feeling a little nervous.

Tera – Rinzee, it's your dream city! Don't be nervous—everything will be great. And don't forget to get a boyfriend; we're in high school now!

I rolled my eyes. Shut up, Tera!

I whispered. Does Joe know that I moved to another city? Did he ask you anything about me?

I'll miss him...

Tera – No, Rinzee, not yet. Actually, I think you should just forget about him and get yourself a new handsome boy, bro.

I sighed. Tera, you know everything about it, and I'm not in a condition to think about it right now.

Forget all these things! For now, I just want to enjoy this beautiful place.

Tera – Okay then! Bye, all the best for your new journey.

[I smile softly] – Thanks, bye!

[Me looking outside the car window, lost in thought.]

[Thinking about Joe...] – I miss you already Joe.

CHAPTER TWO

Memories of Joe

Joe – Zee, did you complete the project Mr. Shylock gave us?

Joe, not yet! Actually, I don't have a teammate yet. Tera and Kam are in the same team, so...

Joe – Why don't we pair up and do the project together?

I – Yeah! Sure, it would be great.

(Back at home, I practically jumped into my room.)

I – Oh my God! I have to clean the room since Joe is coming – yay! What a great day today!

I'm thinking...

Does he like me the same way I like him? Or does he just want to be a good friend? Or is he just using me for the project since I'm a bright student? How will I ever know

what's really on his mind?

(Doorbell rings.)

(I opened the door. Joe is standing there.)

Joe – Hii, Zee!

I – Hello, Joe!

(In my drawing room...)

We were sitting, discussing the project. I wasn't understanding a certain point, so suddenly, he said—

"Hey! Gorgeous Zee! Please try to understand the point."

And I was like... Wait! Wait! Wait! Wait! What did he just call me?

Gorgeous?!

[I blush whenever I think about Joe.]

I – I wish I could be with Joe in this beautiful place... just like his beautiful heart.

Joe – Zee, I want us to be first in this project. And... Zee, I want you to be my friend forever.

[I blushed]

I – Joe, I'm already your friend and will always be! And as for the project, I'm damn sure we'll be first!

(After some time...)

Joe – Now it's time for me to leave.

I – I wish we had a little more time!

Joe – Bye, Zee, my cute friend!

I – Bye, Joe!

Wait! Wait! Wait! Wait! What?! He just called me cute! Aaahhh! What kind of mysteries are these?!

(Joe leaves.)

I send a message to my friends – Hey, I want to tell you something really special!

[In my room – I lay on my bed, thinking about Joe and our project.]

(Next day, at school.)

Mr. Shylock announces the project results—Joe and I are first!

Joe – The credit goes to you, Zee.

I'm thinking...

These are my very first memories with Joe. I found him to be such a nice boy... I never thought that this kind person would turn out to be the most terrible person in my life.

The butterflies in me never noticed the bees around them...

[The car stops! I snapped out of my thoughts.]

CHAPTER THREE

Our New Home

Isabelle Woodrock – See, Rinzee! This is our new house.

I – Nice! *[My eyes widen as I take in the beauty of the house.]*

(The house is beautiful, with a small garden in the front and two balconies.)

(I entered the house and smiled at Mom.)

I – Mum, the house is so nice, and the view from here is amazing!

Noah (Rinzee's younger brother) – Rinzee, my room is bigger than yours!

I'm thinking...

I hope this city brings joy into my life and makes it more beautiful. I just want to forget the past few days... everything that happened.

Joe... Ahh! My mind—no, no, no! Please!

(Next day at the dining table.)

(My family and I are having breakfast.)

Isabelle Woodrock – Don't be nervous Rinzee, you will make new friends here also. And like I said before that things will overcome by the time and the new place will add new energy and new vibes into our life that will help us to keep the back memories on the backside of the almirah of mind. That's why I brought both of you here.

Noah [grinning] – Mum! I'm very excited for this new chapter of life.

Isabelle Woodrock – What about you Rinzee?

I – Hmm, me too.

Isabelle – Good! Kiddo…, I have an event today. Writers from different parts are coming there. Hope it will be good.

Noah and I – All the best, Mum!

Isabelle – Thank you so much, my kiddos…! Love you!

CHAPTER FOUR

First Day, First Friend

(At the school.)

Noah and I enter the school.

I entered the class.

Ms. Shayla Dawson (Rinzee's English teacher) – Welcome, Rinzee!

Dear students, meet your new classmate – Rinzee Woodrock! Nice name, Rinzee.

I – Hello everyone, I'm Rinzee Woodrock. My family has shifted to this beautiful place for some reason, and I hope this new beginning will be great for us. I'm here to have fun, which I think I had lost there. *[press my lips.]* Maybe, this school [moving my shoulder.] brings me joy.

Ms. Shayla Dawson – Rinzee, I've seen your grades. You are a bright student, so don't take any stress. You'll catch up even at mid-semester.

[I take my seat.]

Skye Millar *[smile softly]* – Hi, Rinzee! I'm Skye Millar. You have a cute name, Rinzee.

(The class continues...)

[I get lost in the thoughts of Joe....]

Joe *[locking eyes with me]* – Babe, you look so beautiful. *[leans in closer]*

[I stare into his eyes, feeling my heart race.]

Joe *[softly, just inches away]* – Come closer to me.

[Before I can process it, his lips brush against mine. A kiss. A moment. A flush of warmth between us...]

Joe – *[smiling, pressing a kiss to my forehead]* – I love so much.

(The class ends, snapping me back to reality. I blink, adjusting to my surroundings.)

(Skye and I walk through the school corridor.)

Skye Millar – Rinzee... would you like to be friends with me?

I – Yeah... sure!

Skye Millar – Ms. Shayla Dawson, our English teacher, is really friendly and inspiring. She also has some unique habits—she's always drinking coffee, using fancy words, and being extra passionate about poetry.

I'll tell you more about this school and the personalities of the people here.

[I smile warmly]– Thanks Skye!

Skye Millar – Oh, have you visited Georgiana's famous beach, Geor Beach?

I – Not this time, actually. But I visited it before when I was fifteen. This is my dream city!

Skye Millar – Wow! That sounds amazing. Have you tried the famous cookies from *The Snowy Crumble café.?*

I – Not yet!

Jermey (Skye's friend and classmate) – Hey Skye! Hii Rinzee! Are you coming to the party tonight at Cyrus (Jermey classmate) place?

Skye – Yeah! Of course!

Jermey– What about you, Rinzee?

I – No, no! I don't know anyone here yet, and for me, it's not so easy.

Jermey – But this is a great way to make new friends.

Skye – Yes, Jermey is right! Rinzee, you should come. You'll definitely have fun.

Cyrus (Skye's friend and classmate)– Guys, you're coming, right?

Jermey – Of course! It's going to be a Paaarty!

Skye – Cyrus, invite Rinzee too!

Cyrus *(cool-headed, a bit mysterious, but deeply loyal to his friends)* – Of course! Rinzee, you're most welcome. Don't be boring - please come to the party. Paaarty! Right, bro?

Jermey – Yoo, bro!

(At Isabelle's Writer event.)

Henry Collins(*Classy and sophisticated*) – Hey, Isabelle!

Isabelle – Hi...!

Henry – I'm Henry Collins. I love to read your books.

Isabelle – Thank you so much.

Henry – I'm really happy that I got to meet you. So, what are you writing these days?

Isabelle – I'm currently writing a book on sailing! What about you?

Henry – Well, I just finished writing a mystery novel. So, right now, I'm busy promoting it...!

Isabelle – That's great...!

(And their conversation continues.)

(At the School.)

(At Noah's class.)

Austin *(Noah's classmate)* – Hey, Noah! I'm Austin.

Noah – Hi, Austin!

Austin – Please don't mind me asking, but why did you join in the middle of the session?

Noah – Actually, my parents got divorced, so we shifted here with our mum.

Austin – Oh, I see...! By the way, meet Ryan *(Austin points to his friend and classmate.)*

Ryan – Hey, Noah!

Noah – Hi...!

Ryan*[smirking]* – Don't worry, we'll tell you everything about this school... and its secrets!

Noah *[smile softly]* – Okay!

Austin – I think we're gonna have an amazing vibe together...!

Noah – Yeah...!

Noah – Umm... boys, can I ask you something?

Austin – Sure...!

Noah – What's the name of the girl sitting on that bench?

Austin – Oh, her...! She's **Daisy**. She's sweet and innocent!

Ryan*[smirking]* – Noah, do you have a crush on her?

Noah*[blushing]* – Noo...! It's not like that...!

I just... I just find her really cute. That's all!

Austin *[grinning]* – Ohhh...!

Ryan*[staring at Daisy]* – Everyone finds her cute...!

Austin *[staring at Daisy]* – Yeah, she really is...!

Noah*[surprised]* – Oh... okay...! I think everybody here wants to be her friend.

Ryan*[staring at Daisy]* – Yeah...! I mean, how can someone stop himself from wanting to be her friend?

Noah *[teasingly]* – Bro... something serious?!

Ryan – Noo... no...!

(I went for the next class.)

Mr. Daniel Foster (History teacher) – Oh, you must be the new student. What's your name?

I – Rinzee Woodrock.

Mr. Daniel Foster: That's a nice name. Who gave it to you?

I – My father.

[Me drifts into a memory of my father.]

Ethan Woodrock (Rinzee's father) – Rinzee, I love you, my child. You are my little princess. I will always be with you.

I'm thinking...

You called me a princess... then why did you leave me? Dad, I really miss you...

Jermey – Rinzee, are you coming to the party?

I– I'll think about it.

Jermey – Oh, come on, Rinzee! Just come with us. You'll have fun.

(At my home.)

Isabelle – My kiddos, how was your day?

Noah *[with a big smile on his face.]*

Noah – Great, Mum! I had so much fun. My new school is really good, and I've already made two new friends – **Austin and Ryan.**

Isabelle – That sounds amazing!

Noah – Rinzee, what about you?

Isabelle – Yeah, did you like the school?

I – Yeah, I think it's good.

Noah – Did you make new friends?

[I smiled softly.]

I – Yes! her name is Skye. She seems like a really sweet and cheerful girl. She has this cute and friendly vibe that makes it easy to talk to her. Even though I've just met her, she already feels so welcoming. She's smart, kind, and has a helping nature—like the kind of person who would always be there if you needed something.

Isabelle – That's nice, Rinzee.

I – Skye also invited me to the party at the Cyrus's place.

Isabelle – That's great! You should go. Don't tell me you're thinking of skipping it.

I – Actually, I'm still thinking about it...

Isabelle – No, you're going. Have some fun, honey.

I – Okay! I'll go.

CHAPTER FIVE

The Party at Cyrus's Place

(Me in my room, getting ready for the party.)

I decide to wear a cute black dress. I look in the mirror and realize I look gorgeous.

[I lost into the memory of Joe.]

Joe – Zee, you look so pretty in black, and your smile gives you a natural blush.

[I blush, thinking to myself

It's you who gives me a natural blush...]

(Skye arrives at my home.)

Skye – Hello, Mrs. Woodrock! I'm Skye Millar, Rinzee's friend.

Isabelle – Hi, honey!

Skye – I'm here to pick up Rinzee for the party.

[I come downstairs, ready to leave for the party.]

Isabelle – Oh honey, you look beautiful.

Skye – Yeah, you look really pretty!

I – Really... thank you!

Isabelle – Go girls! Have fun! After all, girls just wanna have fun.

Skye and I say excitedly – Yes...!

(Skye and I leave for the party in Skye's car.)

(At Cyrus' House.)

Jermey – Cyrus, what do you think about Rinzee?

Hannah Carter(a girl from their school) – Rinzee? Hmm, she's a little different. I mean, how can someone just join in the middle of the semester?

Cyrus – Hannah, you can't judge someone like that.

Cyrus – I think she's pretty cool. Once she gets comfortable with us, she'll fit right in.

Hannah – Look who's talking! says the guy who stayed silent for months because of his breakup.

Jermey – Guys, please! Just forget everything. We're at a party—let's enjoy!

Cyrus – Yes! Let's enjoy the paaarty!

Jermey and Cyrus – Oooohhhooo!

(Skye and I reached the party.)

Cyrus, in a loud voice – Hey Skye! Hey, Rinzee!

Skye [*grinned playfully*]– Hi bro! You already started drinking without me?

I smile– Hey, Cyrus.

Cyrus [*looking into Rinzee's eyes.*] - You look pretty!

[I felt a bit shy but stayed calm.] - "Thanks," I said and looked down for a moment.

Cyrus – Rinzee, you know, Jermey and Skye, and I have been friends since we were four.

I – Sounds nice!

Cyrus – So, Rinzee, tell me something about yourself.

I – About me?! I' m a little wild! [*I laugh loudly*] Sorry, just kidding!

Cyrus – [*laughs in surprise*]

[I smiled softly] – Well... I'm Rinzee, I just moved here. I love books, the beach, and... umm... I guess I'm still figuring things out.

Cyrus – Oh, you love books! Nice! What kind of books? Romantic novels?

Me – Umm... maybe, maybe not!

[I glance at Jermey.]

I – Hey, Jermey!

Jermey – Rinzee, I'm happy you came! Umm... you look beautiful!

I – Thanks, Jermey! You're looking good too.

[Jermey smiles, giving a quick blink.]

Jermey – Do you want a drink?

I – No, I don't drink.

Jermey – What! Oh, that's surprising!

I – Actually, I just don't like it.

Jermey – Tell me more things you don't like.

I – But why do you want to know?

Jermey *[with a big smile]* – I... I... I just want to know as a friend.

I – Oh, fine.

Jermey – What did you think huh!

[I smiled] – Nothing, I wasn't thinking about anything.

Skye – Guys, we're playing Never Have I Ever. Would you both like to join?

[Jermey and I exchanged a glance.]

Jermey and Rinzee – Yes!

(In Cyrus' drawing room, the group gathers—Cyrus, Jermey, Skye, Hannah, me, and other friends.)

Cyrus – I'll start. Never have I ever let the past ruin a good party.

[Jermey and Skye exchange glances, but Cyrus just takes a sip like it's no big deal. I noticed but stays quiet, simply observing. A few others take a sip, probably those who have let their past affect them before.]

Hannah – Never have I ever played with someone's feelings.

[Everyone at the party takes a sip.]

Jermey*[looking into Rinzee's eyes]* – Never have I ever moved to a new city and made people curious about me.

[Everyone turns to me, teasing me. I just smile and takes a sip.]

Skye*[with a smile]* – Never have I ever imagined that I could become friends with someone so fast.

[I hugged Skye, making everyone go "Aww."]

I – Never Have I ever dated someone.

[Cyrus and Jermey look at me in surprise.]

Skye – Really?

I – Yeah!

Elena Foster (Hannah's friend and classmate) – She's only saying that to get attention.

Skye – Why you guys have problem with me and my friends? Rinzee hasn't done anything to you, so why are you getting offended by her?

Elena – Fine!

Max (Rinzee's classmate) – Rinzee, don't you have a crush on someone?

I – No, it's not like that!

Skye – So you do have a crush on someone?

[Everyone waits for my response.]

I – Umm... like, I have!

Skyeand Max – Who's that lucky guy?

I – Guys, actually, I can't tell you right now.

Cyrus – Come on, Rinzee! You can tell us.

Skye – Yeah, Rinzee!

Jermey – Rinzee, only if you're comfortable. Don't feel pressured.

I – Thanks, Jermey! For understanding me.

Skye – Okayyy, enough with the secrets! Let's wrap up the game before things get too serious.

Cyrus – Yeah, let's do something fun now!

[Just as everyone starts thinking about what to do next, someone glances at the time.]

Hannah – Woah, guys! It's already late.

Max – Yeah, I didn't even realize how fast time flew.

Skye – Ugh, I don't wanna leave yet, but I guess we should.

I – Yeah, it was fun though!

Jermey – Let's do this again sometime!

(Everyone agrees, exchanging quick goodbyes before heading toward the door. Skye and I left together, chatting about the night as we got into the car.)

Skye – Come Rinzee, I'll drop you!

I – Okay! Let's go!

(Skye and I wave goodbye to everyone and head to the car. As they drive through the quiet streets of Georgiana, the cold breeze makes the night feel even more refreshing.)

[At the Jermey's home, he sits on the balcony, lost in thought.]

Jermey*[thinking, gazing at the stars]*: How can someone be so beautiful?

[His mind drifts, words forming in his head like a quiet melody.]

"She used to like the way I like her.

She used to like the way I called her.

She used to like the way I imagine her.

She used to like the way I create us.

She used to like the way I melt for her.

She used to like the way I long for her.

She used to like the way I am attracted to her.

She used to like the way I miss her.

She used to like the way I listen to her.
She used to like the way I wish for her.
She used to like the way I admire her.
She used to like the way I liked her—only that."

This moon understands my words, listens without judgment, without thinking how weird I am, without offering any solutions. Even the silence between us feels so beautiful, so pure—so full of unspoken sharing. Or maybe... the moon already knows my mood, the purity of my heart. Haahaa, ironically, I'm as close to you as you are far from me.

And yet, as I sit here, lost in thoughts of her, I find myself speaking to the moon instead. Because this moon understands my words... and I know you will never just abandon me. Never....

(In the car, Skye leans back, smirking at me...)

Skye – Rinzee... tell me, who is your crush?

I – Skye! Not now.

[I look outside the window, lost in thought.] I wish Joe was with me tonight...

Skye – Rinzee! What are you thinking about?

I – Joe...

Skye – Who?

I – Nothing! Just about tomorrow's school day.

Skye – Uh-huh, sure. *[She smirks but doesn't push me further.]*

(Skye pulls up in front of my house.)

Skye – Here you go, home safe!

I – Thanks, Skye! Tonight was fun.

Skye – Always!

(I entered my home.)

Isabelle – How was your party, honey? Did you Enjoy it?

[I smile brightly]– It was fun! Yes, I enjoyed the party.

[As I lay on my bed, I kept thinking about the party.]
Skye is such a nice girl.
[I think Jermey is really understanding!]
By the way, Cyrus is nice to... but why did Hannah have a problem with me?
Maybe there's something from the past related to Skye.
Well, tonight was fun!
Rinzee... Georgiana is going to be fun...

CHAPTER SIX

New Friendships and Old Secrets

(The next day, at school.)

Jermey – Hey, Cyrus! Yesterday was fun, right?

Cyrus – Yeah, bro!

Jermey – Did you see Rinzee?

Cyrus – Hmm... bro, what's the scene?

Jermey – Nothing! Just casually asking!

Max – Did Rinzee come?

[Jermey and Cyrus exchange glances and laugh.]

Max – What happened?

Cyrus – Nothing!

Skye – Hey, guys!

Jermey – Hey, Skye! Did you prepare for the test?

Skye – Yeah, bro!

(As I arrived at school, I saw Skye waiting for me.)

Skye – Hey, Rinzee! Did you know about today's test?

[I surprised] – What! A test?

Skye – Oh no, Rinzee! Mr. Graves, our French teacher, is **très strict!** If you mispronounce a word, he'll stare at you like you've committed a crime. And don't even think about using Google Translate for homework—he always knows.

I – Wow, sounds intense. I'm doomed.

Jermey – Don't stress, Rinzee!

Cyrus – Yeah, just tell him you're a new student.

I – Okay, I'll try!

(In the classroom.)

Mr. Graves – Students, think carefully before handing in a bad test—because you know the rest. (glances around) Oh! A new student! Your previous school had French as a subject, I assume?

I – Uh... yes!

Mr. Graves – Good. Then no excuses. All the best, everyone!

(After the test, in the corridor)

Jermey – How was your test, Rinzee?

I – Not too bad... but not great either.

Jermey – If you want, I can teach you French.

Skye – Yes! You know, Rinzee, Jermey's French is actually outstanding. That's why he's Mr. Graves' favourite student!

I – Oh, that's great! Jermey, will you please teach me? *[in a cute voice]*

Jermey *[with a small smile]* – Of course, Rinzee!

I – So, 5 PM at my place?

Jermey*[grinning]* – Okay!

Cyrus – What's going on, guys?

I – Cyrus, you know Jermey will teach me French.

Cyrus – Oh! That's nice!

Natalie Pierce(*Classy, confident, and knows how to play mind games)* – Hey, Cyrus! I think we need to talk.

Cyrus – No, I don't think so. Please stay away from me!

I – Skye, who is that girl?

Skye – Natalie Pierce—Cyrus' ex! And, by the way, she and Hannah are best friends.

I – What?! There are so many complications.

[In my mind – Oh, now I understand why Hannah is so rude to me and Skye. But then why did Hannah come to the party? At Cyrus' place? Wow!]

I – Skye, then why did she come to the party?

Skye – Before Cyrus and Natalie started dating, Cyrus, Natalie, Hannah, and I were all friends. Hannah had promised Cyrus that her friendship with Natalie wouldn't come in between them. That's why she came to the party.

I – And because of that, she hates us? But why?

Skye – She hates me because I told Cyrus to break his friendship with Hannah! And since you're my friend, she probably doesn't like you either.

I – Oh, so she thinks like this! Okay!

[As Natalie left, I glanced at Cyrus. He looked annoyed, rubbing his thumb against his finger. And for a second—just a second—his eyes met mine. Something about the way he looked at me made my heart skip a beat. But before I could even process it, he looked away.]

CHAPTER SEVEN

First Lessons, First Spark

(At my home.)

I'm thinking...

I was thinking about my day at school. I'm unaware of so many secrets among them. And... I think Cyrus is a very mysterious person.

(Doorbell rings.)

[Noah opens the door. Jermey is standing there.]

Noah –Yes?

Jermey – Hey, I'm Jermey! Rinzee's friend.

Noah – Oh! Come in, please! Rinzee, come here—Jermey is here!

(I come downstairs.)

Jermey *(looking into Rinzee's eyes)* – Hey, Rinzee!

[I smile softly] – Hey, Jermey! What would you like to have?

Jermey – Nothing!

I – Don't be formal! I'll bring you a cold coffee.

(After some time...)

[Jermey is teaching me French.]

Jermey – Rinzee, am I a good teacher? I mean, are you getting me?

I – Yes, of course!

[*Jermey is staring at me, thinking—Wow, she is so beautiful. Her cute voice... her eyes have some kind of power that pulls me toward her.*]

Jermey – Rinzee, I want to say something to you.

I – Yes?

Jermey – Rinzee, you know... umm... nothing!

I – Come on, Jermey! Just say it!

Jermey – No, no, it's nothing!

I – Jermey, don't be like this! How do I say it?

Jermey – Okay... Rinzee, you have such a beautiful voice. You can pull anyone toward you with your voice.

[I stare at him in surprise, my cheeks heating up.] – What?

Jermey [*shrugging with a smile*] – It's true...!

I – Yeah, right! If that were the case, someone would have been impressed by me by now!

Jermey – I don't know why it hasn't happened yet, but you really do have such a nice voice.

[I blush softly] – Thank you so much, Jermey!

Jermey – Rinzee, let's focus on studying now. I don't want you to get distracted because of me.

I – It's not like that!

(After some time...)

Jermey – By the way, Rinzee, why haven't you dated anyone?

I – Umm... maybe I just haven't found the right one.

Jermey – What does love mean to you?

[*I press my lips together, shrugging.*] – Well, I think...
maybe it sounds foolish, but...
It's not "I love you."
It's "I want to love you."
And that one line sums up what love means to me.

[Jermey takes a deep breath, his eyes locking onto mine, quietly studying me.] –

Jermey - Rin... you're amazing. You have such a beautiful heart.

[My eyes smiles as I blink, placing my palms gently on my cheeks.]

I – Umm...hmm...!

Jermey*[smirking]* – What's stopping you? Or... are you just afraid to fall for it?

[I shrugged, a little nervous.] Ann... it's not like something's stopping me, but... but... but... maybe I'm afraid to fall for it!

Please don't ask what.

Jermey*[glances to the side, sensing her unease]* – Umm... okay.

(A gentle silence settles between us.)
Jermey – Rinzee, it's time for me to go.

I – Umm... yeah.

Jermey – Okay then! See you at school—and here too. What time should I come tomorrow?

I – Same time!

Jermey [teasingly] – Bye, Rin...!

[A slight blush creeps up as I tease him back, feeling a flutter in my chest.]– Bye, Jer...!

CHAPTER EIGHT

Evening Glances

(In the evening, at the park.)

(Noah and Austin are there.)

Noah – Austin, look... that's Daisy, right?

Austin – Yeah...!

Noah – Come on, let's talk to her.

Austin – Okay...!

Noah[smile softly] – Hey, Daisy!

Daisy[smile warmly] – Hi! What a pleasant surprise!

Noah – So, do you come here daily to the park?

Daisy – Yeah, I usually come with my dog, Demmy, for a walk.

Noah – Oh, that's nice...!

Austin – Noah, it's getting late for me! so I'll take your leave!

Noah – Okay...! Then, bye...!

Daisy – You come daily too?

Noah – Yeah, mostly for a walk... or sometimes to play! By the way, you're really sweet...!

Daisy[smiling shyly] – Oh, thanks...!

Daisy – Please don't mind, but it's getting a bit late for me too. So... can we walk home together?

Noah[smiling softly] – Yeah, sure....!

(Next day, at home.)

Isabelle – Rinzee, Noah told me that your friend came over yesterday!

[In my mind – Why does Noah tell everything to Mum?!]

I – Yeah, he came here to teach me French.

Isabelle – That's nice! You're making new friends.

[I start thinking about Jermey and blush.]

Isabelle – Rinzee... hmm... hmm... blushing and all? What's the scene, Rinzee?

I – Nothing, Mum! He's just my friend.

Noah – Oh, "just a friend"? But I heard him tell you that you have a nice voice and can attract anyone with it!

Isabelle*[teasingly]* – That's nice! Someone is getting attracted to my daughter...

[I blush and feel a little shy] – No, Mum! He's just a friend!

Isabelle – We'll see!

I'm thinking...

Mum is always the chill one. She never controls me, and she even teases me for things that have or haven't happened. But Dad... he never wanted me to date anyone in high school. After we separated from him, I think I can finally date freely. But... is Mum right? Does Jermey like me?

Noah – Come on, Rinzee! We're getting late.

I – Yeah...

CHAPTER NINE

Natalie and Past Shadows

(At school.)

Cyrus – Hey, girls!

I & Skye – Hi!

Natalie Pierce*(placing her hand on his shoulder.)* – Hey, Cyrus! Just listen to me once. Just once, please!

Cyrus*(pulling away.)* – I don't want to talk to you. And don't you dare touch me again. Actually, I wish I could erase the memory of your touch from my mind.

Natalie – Cyrus, please! Skye, please tell him to just listen to me once!

Skye – I am not saying a single word between both of you. Don't drag me into this again.

Natalie – Please, Skye! Not because you're my friend, but because of your humanity.

Cyrus – Skye, don't say a single word. Natalie, you should have thought about this before you cheated on me. And now, suddenly, you're saying all this?

Natalie – I know I made a big mistake. And I'm sorry for that. I'm sorry for everything I've done to you.

Cyrus – Oh... and why am I even listening to this? Just stay away from me!

[Cyrus walks away. I silently watch this whole dramatic scene unfold, and in my mind, I'm like—Wow, Rinzee, what kind of friends have you made? With new friends, comes new drama too!]

Natalie – Skye, I was your friend, and yet you didn't say a single word?!

Skye – Yeah, exactly—as you said, I **was** your friend. Now, I can't even stand your double face.

[Skye grabs my hand.]

Skye – Rinzee, let's go!

[I'm shocked] – Skye, what just happened? Can you please tell me the whole story?!

Skye – Firstly, Rinzee, remember one thing—you need to stay away from Natalie and her group. Second, as you already know, Natalie was Cyrus' ex. She cheated on Cyrus with Ryder Hayes—a smooth talker, flirty, and a little manipulative. She was kind of double-dating both of them. And since Ryder doesn't care about anything except having a girl, he didn't mind. He's quite famous in school for his endless dating and so-called relationships.

I – Oh, now she wants Cyrus back!

Skye – But Cyrus won't give her another chance. He already did once, and she misused it badly.

I – But why did Natalie cheat on Cyrus? I mean, what was the reason?

Skye – Cyrus says that Natalie got bored of him. She didn't want to be with a guy who was always there for her—too caring, too loyal, never did anything wrong that could affect their relationship. Basically, she said she wanted some drama in her life.

I – What...! Oh, what kind of girl is she?! How can someone leave such a nice person?

Skye – Yeah...! She's a total dumbo...! You know, Rinzee, Cyrus was so in love with her that after the breakup, he became completely silent. He didn't even talk to me or Jermey. We were very tensed for him at that time.

I – Then why does she want him back now?

Skye – You're right!

Jermey – Skye! What was everyone talking about? Was that bitch Natalie begging Cyrus to talk to her?

Skye – Yeah!

Jermey – Where is Cyrus?

Skye – I don't know.

Jermey – Then we should go find him.

I – Sorry for interrupting! But I think we should leave him alone for some time.

Jermey – Yes, you're right! He might feel better.

Skye – But...! Okay. Then let's go home!

I – Jermey, will you come today to teach me?

Jermey – Yes, of course!

CHAPTER TEN

New Vibes, New Confessions

(At my home.)

Noah – Rinzee, is that guy coming again to teach you?

I – Yes!

Noah*[teasingly.]* – That's nice! What was his name again? Ann... Jermey, right?

I – Yes, his name is Jermey. But why are you so interested in knowing all of this?

Noah*[smirking]* – I'm just asking because I'm your brother...!

I – You think I'm dumb?!

Noah – No, no...!

(Noah runs away laughing.)

[In my room, I lie on my bed, chatting with Tera and Kam. I'm telling them about this beautiful and—honestly—dramatic place.]

(Doorbell rings.)

(I open the door. Jermey is standing there.)

Jermey – Hey, Rinzee! I'm backkkkk.

[I smile softly.] – Yes, welcomeeee!

(In my room.)

Jermey – Rinzee, why are we studying in your room today?

I – So that nobody can listen to what we're talking about.

[In a louder voice.] Because some people in this house love to eavesdrop on things that have nothing to do with them!

Jermey [confused] – What are you talking about?

I – Nothing, Jermey! Let's just study.

Jermey – Okay...!

(After some time.)

I – Can I ask you something?

Jermey – Yes, of course!

I – As you already know, Hannah and Natalie don't like me at all. But I wasn't even there when Cyrus and Natalie broke up. So why do they dislike me?

Jermey – It's very simple, Rinzee. Since you're friends with me, Skye, and Cyrus, you automatically become a rival to them.

[I'm surprised.] – Rival...?! But there's nothing between Cyrus and me.

Jermey – Yeah! We know that. But they might think otherwise... and there's a reason behind it.

I – What reason?

Jermey – Since I'm telling you a secret, first promise me that you won't tell anyone you know about it.

[I blink.]– Okay...! I won't tell anyone.

Jermey – There was a time when Skye liked Cyrus... but Cyrus didn't feel the same way.

[I'm shocked.]– What...?!

Jermey – Yes! Skye confessed her feelings to him...

[My eyes widen.]– And Cyrus rejected her?!

Jermey – Yeah, Rinzee! Cyrus liked Natalie, who was Skye's friend. But Skye handled the situation really well—she friend-zoned herself and slowly moved on. Since Cyrus and Natalie liked each other, they started dating.

I – Wow... Skye has such a big heart! I love her.

[Jermey smiles softly]

[I roll my lips.] – Jermey, it feels like everyone here has some kind of past.

Jermey – Rinzee, it's not about the place. Everyone has a past—something they're either afraid to talk about or too scared to accept. Life chooses the path for us.

I – Yeah, you're right.

Jermey – I think our past helps us understand life and its phases. Every day, every minute, every second—they're all like teachers. They teach us little things that make it easier to understand the big changes in life.

I – Yeah, our past guides us, preparing us for the real movie of life.

Jermey*[teasing smile]* – Oh, wow... a movie, huh?

[I smirk.] – Sometimes, I talk like you too.

(Meanwhile, at the beachside...)

(Cyrus was sitting there, lost in thought about everything that had happened today.)

Cyrus [thinking]: Why does Natalie want me back now? Didn't she say she wanted drama in her life? Or is she just trying to make Ryder jealous by using me? Maybe now she's taking revenge on Ryder...

I think I'm done with her. Completely.

In fact... I don't even want to date anyone anymore. I've decided—I won't.

(The next morning, at school...)

Noah*[nervously]* – Daisy would you like to go to Snowy Crumble café with me this evening?

Daisy[*shrugging with smile*] – Umm... Yes!

Skye[*grinning*] – Hey, Rinzee! How are your home classes going? [*teasingly*]I mean... is your new smart, handsome, and hot teacher teaching you properly?

[I smile softly.]– Yeah, I think he's quite understanding too.

Skye – Yes, you're right! Jermey is a very understanding and genuine person.

I – And, of course, he's good at French too.

Skye[*smirking*] – But Rinzee! He's smart, hot, and handsome too.

Jermey – Hey, beautiful girls! What are you talking about?

Skye & Rinzee – Hi, Jermey!

Me – We are talking about you. Jer...Jer... may...!

Jermey [*blushing in surprise*] – Woah... Woah... Rinzee!

Skye [*teasingly*] – Oh... some nerdy things are happening here!

[I smile softly.] – No, Skye! It's just like... a vibe-match kind of thing.

Jermey – Yeah...!

Skye[*smirking*] – Okay...!

Max – Hey, guys! Did you hear what happened last night?

Jermey, Skye, and I[*surprised*] – No! What happened?!

Max – Natalie went to Cyrus's house and literally begged him to talk to her. And guess what? She even uploaded a video of it on social media to get sympathy from her followers.

[I'm shocked.] – What...?!

Skye & Jermey[*angrily*] – We knew it! We knew she wouldn't stop there. She was going to do something big... and here it is!

Skye – Show me the video!

Max(*showing the video of Natalie*) –

(In the video – Natalie rings the doorbell of Cyrus's house. Cyrus opens the door, and she immediately starts begging.)

"Please, baby, give me a second chance! I love you! I'm sorry for everything that happened!"

(But Cyrus, without saying a single word, shuts the door in her face!)

Jermey[*grinning, shaking his head*] – Woah... Woah...! My boy handled it RIGHT!

Skye (*grinning*) – Cyrus did an amazing job!

I – Yeah, Cyrus literally gave her that "just go, bitch!" attitude! Wow!

Max – You know, because of this video, Natalie is actually getting what she wanted—*"sympathy."* Everyone's saying Cyrus should give her a second chance.

Jermey – I don't think Cyrus will. After what he did yesterday, it's clear he doesn't give a fuck about her anymore.

Skye [roll her lips.] – Yeah, you're right! But wow... Natalie, what have you done?! All this drama... just for sympathy.

[I rub my forehead.] – Yeah...! What kind of girl is she?!

Jermey – Rinzee, you've only seen Natalie's behaviour—that was just the trailer. Once you see Hannah's side of things... *[He shakes his head]* Oh god...!

Max – Yes, Rinzee! You should stay away from them. Who knows? Maybe their next target is you.

[My eyebrows shoot up.] – What...?!

Jermey – Don't be scared, Rinzee. We're here to protect you.

Skye – Yes! Don't worry!

I'm thinking...

Wow... all the best, Rinzee. More drama is on the way. Get ready!

Cyrus – Hey, guys! What's up?!

(Everyone in school is staring at him, whispering and gossiping.)

Cyrus – So, who care about everyone. I don't give anything about anyone except my special people.

I – Hi, Cyrus! We know what happened last night.

Cyrus[*in a sassy voice*]– Oh, so... do you also think I should give her a second chance?

(Jermey, Skye, Cyrus, and Max all wait for my response.)

I – No, not at all!

Jermey – We all think you did an amazing job, and you don't have to give a fuck about her.

Cyrus[*puts his hand on Jermey's shoulder*] – Yo, bro...!

Max – But now what?

Skye – What do you mean, Max?

Max – I mean, now everyone will think that Cyrus was too harsh with Natalie.

Cyrus – So? Who cares about *"everyone"*? I don't give a damn about anyone except my special people.

Skye[*smiling softly*] – What a change, Cyrus!

Max – Yeah, honestly... I thought after all this drama, you might give her another chance!

I – No way! She doesn't deserve it!

Max – Guys, can I make a request?

Jermey – Yes, bro!

Max – As you guys already know... I don't really have friends in school. So... can I join your group?

(Jermey, Skye, Cyrus, and I exchange glances... then all of us smile softly.)

Jermey & Cyrus – Yes, bro! Of course!

Skye[*in a warning voice*] – But don't you dare share any of our secrets... otherwise!

Max – Yeah, I promise! I won't spill any of your secrets!

I – Where's Natalie?

Max – She's absent today.

[*I tease him, grinning.*] – Max, can I call you *Crime Master Googo?* Since you always have all the gossip!

Max[*laughing loudly*] – Yeah, Rinzee! You can...!

Jermey – You've chosen a very good name, Rinzee!

CHAPTER ELEVEN

A Glimpse of Daisy

(At the Snowy Crumble café.)

Noah *[gazing at her]* – Daisy, you know... you're the first girl, I've ever found this cute and sweet.

Daisy*[looking down with a smile]* – Oh... Noah, thank you... thank you! And by the way, you're really smart too.

Noah*[thinking to himself]* – Should I tell her now? Umm... no... no... not yet...

(After some time... They step out of the Snowy Crumblecafé, the evening air cool and calm.)

(Noah and Daisy walks side by side, their arms lightly brushing as they stroll through the quiet streets.)

[Daisy glances at Noah, then looks away with a tiny smile.]

(Noah, a little nervous, lets his hand swing close to hers. Their fingers gently brush once... then again... until finally—)

(Their pinkies hook, just barely, but enough.)

Daisy*[softly, almost whispering]* – I never thought a walk like this could feel this nice.

Noah *[smiling, looking at her]* – Me neither.

(They keep walking, fingers still linked, the silence between them warm and comfortable.)

CHAPTER TWELVE

The Kiss and the Storm

(After school, at home.)

[I lie on my bed, thinking...]

Today, I have friends who feel like home. But...

Tera and Kam have completely forgotten me. They don't even read my messages.

So... Rinzee, it's happening again—ghosting. Why, God? Why always me?

Every time I consider someone special, after all the amazing moments we share... they ghost me.

[in a taunting voice] Congratulations, Rinzee! You lose. Another loss. Once again.

(Doorbell rings.)

(Isabelle Opens the door, Jermey is standing there.)

Isabelle – Yes?

Jermey – Hello, I'm Jermey, Rinzee's friend!

Isabelle *[smiling softly]* – Oh...! so you're the one I've been hearing about these days.

Jermey *[smiling in surprise]* – Yeah, I guess I'm the one!

Isabelle – Please, come in, kiddo!

Noah – Hi, Jermey!

Jermey – Hi, Cham!

Noah[*teasingly*] – Will you be teaching her in her room again today?

Jermey[*in a shy voice*] – I don't know... whatever Rinzee prefers.

Isabelle[*in a slightly teasing voice*]– Noah, don't say it like that!

Jermey – Where's Rinzee?

Isabelle – Oh, I forgot to call her.

(Isabelle calls Rinzee.)

I'm thinking...

Oh God... I completely forgot to tell Jermey not to come today! Now, Mum is going to tease me so much!

Isabelle – Jermey, what would you like to have?

Noah – Mum, please make your special Alfredo Pasta!

I – Yes, Mum! Please...!

Isabelle – Okay! But does Jermey like it too?

Jermey – Yeah, I like it too...

(Jermey and I are studying in my room.)

I'm thinking...

Damn... Jermey looks so hot and handsome.

Jermey [*thinking*]:*Damn, she's so beautiful and cute. I wish she were mine.*

Jermey[*staring at me*] – Rinzee, you look so beautiful.

[*I'm smiling.*]– Thanks, Jermey! Today was full of drama.

Jermey – Yeah...!

I'm thinking...

Oh God! Why is he staring at me like that?!

I– Jermey, what are you thinking?

Jermey – Nothing!

(We move closer...)

Jermey(*moving even closer*) – Oh, Rinzee... I wish...!

I'm thinking....

Jermey...!
[And then... Jermey and I kiss.]
(Suddenly, the door swings open.)
My Father – "Rinzee, my princess—"
(He walks in... right in the middle of our kiss.)
Ethan Woodrock (Rinzee's Father) *[in angrily louder voice.]* – Rinzee, what is this...?!
Jermey – Sir, sir...! I can explain...! This is a misunderstanding!
Ethan – No, just shut up! I'm not talking to you!
I – No, Dad! It's not what you think!
Ethan – I told you—NO dating in high school!
(Isabelle rushes upstairs after hearing the loud voices.)
Isabelle – What's going on here?!
Ethan – Is this how you're taking care of my kids?!
Isabelle – What happened?!
I – Mum, this is just a misunderstanding!
Ethan – Just shut up, Rinzee!
Jermey – Sir, please... just listen to us first!
Ethan – Isabelle, tell me—did you know what she was doing?!
Isabelle*[angrily]* – *Yeah, I know! And WHY do you always try to force your decisions on others?!*
I – Mum... we were just kissing!
Isabelle – You don't have to give me any justification. You're free to do anything... like a bird.
Isabelle*(making eye contact with Ethan)* – *Come on, kids. Let's go downstairs.*
(In the drawing room.)
Jermey – Mrs. Woodrock, it was just a moment. We're not dating right now.
Isabelle – Jermey, I know. You don't have to justify anything to me. Even if you two were dating, I'd be happy

for you both because I know Rinzee would make the right choice.

[I hug Mum tightly.]– Thank you so much! I love you.

Isabelle – I love you too, my kiddo!

Jermey – You're so understanding, Mrs. Woodrock!

Isabelle – *Thanks, Jermey!*

Jermey – I think... I should leave now.

I – I'm so sorry, Jermey... for everything that happened here.

Jermey – No, no... Rinzee! Don't be.

(Jermey and I step outside my house.)

Jermey – Rinzee, what happened today is one thing... but what I told you—that was real.

I – Hmm... Jermey...

Jermey – I know... it's not the right time. So maybe later, I will...!

Jermey – Bye, Rinzee! See you tomorrow at school!

I – Yeah...!

(I enter my home. My parents are fighting.)

[I silently walk to my room.

Tears start falling from my eyes.]

Why... why does Dad always do this to me?

He always wants me to walk on the path he chose for me...

Even after we moved here, he just wants to ruin our peace.

[angrily] What's his problem?!

I just hate him...!

I don't want to love you anymore!

(I check my phone. There's a message from Jermey—)

Jermey –Rinzee, are you alright?

Why... why is this person so nice?

I want him, but... my fear.

[in a frustrated voice] – *No... no, Rinzee! Not this time!*

Aann... what should I do now?

Should I tell him about my past? Or just go with the flow?

Jermey is such a nice guy... and he's so understanding. He would definitely understand me.

But...!

[I grab my pillow and scream into it.] – *No... no... no!!!*

(After some time...)

(Mum walks into my room.)

Isabelle – Kiddo...!

[In a shaky voice, tears in my eyes] – Mum...! Why does Dad always do this to us?!

Isabelle – I told you, you don't have to worry. Just do whatever you want—you are free, my child!

I – *I love you, Mum!*

Isabelle – I love you too!

I – When will Dad leave? I don't want him to stay!

Isabelle– Rinzee, don't say that! But... I'll try my best to make sure he doesn't stay for long.

I – Where's Noah?

Isabelle – He's gone to his friend's house to do his homework.

I – At least he's safe from all this drama.

Isabelle – For now, just sleep, and don't overthink! Good night!

I – Mum... please stay with me forever.

Isabelle – Always.

I – Good night!

(Noah comes back home.)

(He sees his father.)

Ethan[*smiling*] – Noah...! How are you?

Noah – Why are you here?

Ethan – What...?! Don't you even like meeting me?

Noah – Meeting you? Honestly, I don't even like you.

Isabelle – Noah, you're back! How was it?

Noah – Good...! Mum, why is Dad here?

Ethan – So, you're telling my kids not to even like me?

Isabelle[*angrily*] – Please...! You are responsible for this. If they don't like you, it's because of YOU!

Ethan – What have I done?

Isabelle – Think!

(Ethan is sitting in the drawing room.)

(Isabelle walks in.)

Ethan – Do you really think I'm responsible for all this?

Isabelle – Yes...! You are!

Ethan – You know the reason why I don't want Rinzee to date in high school.

Isabelle – Ethan, situations don't always stay the same. Just because you went through something doesn't mean our child will face it too.

Ethan – Isabelle, you know I'm just being protective!

Isabelle – No, no! You're not protecting her—you're forcing her to walk on a path you chose for her!

Ethan – But...!

Isabelle – You have to let them learn from their own mistakes. Let them enjoy their journey of life, just like we did.

Kids should be free, like birds...! Let them find their own nest, their own sky.

Ethan – But as parents, we have to protect them too, right?

Isabelle – Yes, we should protect them... but not at the cost of their freedom.

Ethan – Isabelle, I don't want my kids to go through the same pain I went through.

Isabelle – As parents, we can guide them toward the right path... but we can't choose it for them.

Ethan – Our thoughts never match!

Isabelle – They did once. But now, I don't even want you in my life!

Ethan[*angrily*] – Isabelle, I don't know why you all are so different!

Isabelle – We're not different. You just have an orthodox mindset and force your decisions on others.

Ethan – Fine! I don't want to stay here anymore.

Isabelle[*folding her arms*] – Okay...!

CHAPTER THIRTEEN

Goodbye to Chains

(Ethan storms out of the house.)

Isabelle – Thank God! He left...!

(Isabelle's thoughts:)

I don't want my kids to even meet him again!

He's just... ahh!

[in a relaxing voice] *– Finally... end of this drama!*

(Meanwhile, Jermey at his home.)

(Jermey lies on his bed, lost in thought.)

Jermey *[thinking]: After what happened yesterday, will Rinzee still continue our friendship?*

I like her, and I don't want to lose her!

She sees me as someone understanding, so I hope she doesn't think I wouldn't understand...

(He grabs his phone to check—did she reply? But she didn't.)

Will she even want to talk? Damn, why am I overthinking this?

(Isabelle calls Henry.)

Isabelle*[in a breaking voice]* – I want to meet you right now!

Henry – Right now?!

Isabelle – Yeah, please...!

(At the Café.)

Henry – Tell me, Isabelle, what happened?

Isabelle*[in a breaking voice]* – My husband...!

(Isabelle breaks down and tells him everything that happened.)

Henry*[softly]* – Hey... hey...! You just... don't worry, Isabelle.

I'm here for you – whenever you need something, someone to just listen to you.

Isabelle*[wiping her tears]* – Thank you so much, Henry...!

Henry – Just remember one thing – I'll be always be there for you, my Issaaa...!

Isabelle*[touched]* – Oh, Henry! It really means a lot...!

CHAPTER FOURTEEN

A Brave Heart Awakens

(Next morning...)

(We are sitting at the dining table.)

I – Did Dad leave?

Isabelle – Yes.

I – Last night?

Isabelle – Yes.

Noah – Aren't you happy about it?

I – I mean... I am! But...?

Noah – You should be, Rinzee!

Isabelle – Kiddo, don't say that. After all, he's still your dad.

Noah – Dad? More like a ringmaster!

[I laugh.]– Yeah, you're right!

Isabelle – Kids, you're getting late for school!

I – Mum, after what happened last night... how am I supposed to face Jermey?

Isabelle – Rinzee, Jermey is a very understanding person. So don't worry!

I – Mum, should I tell everyone about my past? That I've dated Joe and got badly cheated by him.

Isabelle – Yeah, you should! If you don't, then where's the honesty in building any bond?

Rin, you should be honest with everyone. You should never be afraid to share anything that's related to you.

Just... be my brave girl, okay!

[I smile softly.] – Okay, mum...!

[thinking]:

I'll tell them...

But not now...

Maybe after some time...

A Shoulder to Lean On

(At school.)

Cyrus – Hey, Rinzee!

[I reply in a low voice.] – Hi, Cyrus.

Cyrus – What's wrong? I mean... why do you sound so low?

Skye – Hi, guys!

Cyrus – Yo, bro!

Skye – What happened, Rinzee? Is everything alright?

Cyrus – Yeah, you look really down.

Skye – Yeah...! Come on, Rinzee. You can share with us.

Cyrus – Wait a second...! Did Natalie say something to you?

I – No...!

Skye – Then what happened?

I – First, tell me, where's Jermey?

Cyrus – He's at the playground.

I – Okay, I'll meet you guys after I meet Jermey.

Skye – Okay, Rinzee!

(I walked toward the playground, my heart racing a little...)

I'm thinking....

I hope Jermey doesn't feel awkward talking to me, now.

I really want him as my friend… or maybe even my future boyfriend.

Ahh…! I hate my mind! Oh, sorry…! I just love you, baby!

But please, for now, don't bring such thoughts.

(I walk toward the playground, my heart beating a little faster.)

[I spot Jermey sitting with his friends, but he seems lost in thought. His eyes are unfocused, like he's somewhere else entirely.]

I– Jermey, can we talk?

Jermey– Yeah, sure…!

I – Sorry… for all that drama.

Jermey – I told you, don't be…! I also want to tell you something.

[Surprised, I reply.]– Okay…!

Jermey[*Hesitating*] – Rinzee…I –!

[I blink.] – Huh?

Jermey [*forcing a smile*] – Never mind… let's go.

(Jermey and I walk toward our class. I keep my eyes on the ground, lost in thought.)

Jermey – Rinzee, why do you seem so distant?

[I snap out of my thoughts and shake my head quickly.]

I – No, nothing…!

(Jermey stops walking and looks at me, tilting his head slightly.)

Jermey – Rinzee… you can tell me. I won't judge you. **I'm thinking….**

I press my lips together, my chest tightening. Can I really tell him? Will he even understand?

Okay, I've decided—I will tell him.

I – Jermey, there's a reason why my dad reacted that way yesterday.

Jermey – Okay, tell me…!

I – Actually, there's a long story behind this.

Jermey[*smiling softly*] – I'm ready to hear your long story...!

(*I take a deep breath before continuing.*)

I – When my dad was in high school, he dated someone. In the beginning, she was really sweet and pretty.

My dad was so in love with her that he couldn't even see the bees around him.

Jermey [*pressing his lips together*]– That's why he...

[I brink.] – Yeah...

And after four years of their relationship, she made false allegations against my dad because she wanted to end things. That's why she did it.

Jermey[*surprised*] – What...?!

I – Yeah, after the breakup, my dad was in depression for so long. My mum was the one who helped him come out of it.

And my mum and dad fell in love with each other, so they got married.

Jermey[*moving his eyes and brows*] – Your mum became an angel for him.

I – That's the reason he doesn't want me to have a boyfriend in high school. He doesn't want me to go through the same situation, the same pain as him.

[Jermey takes a deep breath.]

I – But my mum always wanted me to decide for my own life. To choose my own path, because it gives me the strength to understand this beautiful life.

She always tells me that whatever happened with dad is a part of his life, not mine...!

He went through so much pain, but he also learned so much from it.

Jermey *[holds my hand into his]* – Rinzee, somewhere, your dad's reaction makes sense from his perspective.

He's been through so much... all those false allegations, oh God...!

But your mom is right too. We have to choose our own path, our own journey.

Don't worry, Rinzee! Just do whatever feels right...!

[I nod appreciatively] – Thank you so much, Jermey! For understanding me...!

Jermey – Oh, Rinzee...! It's okay...!

Can I call you Rin?

I – Of course...!

Jermey *[teasingly]* – Rin... rin...!

[I smile softly.]

Jermey– Oh, by the way, what's the meaning of your name?

[I beam.] – It means a '***rare star***'.

Jermey *[grinning]* – Wow... That suits you.

[I blush a little, looking away.]

Jermey – Rin... after this long, crazy *[smirks]* thing, why don't you come over for dinner? My mom would love to meet you.

[I blink.] – Yeah, sure! *[stares at Jermey and narrows my eyes]* – Meet me?

Jermey*[smiling, pressing his lips together]* – Yeah... *[furrows his brows slightly]* – You'll know when you meet her.

[I frowned, confused.] – Okay...!

(We head to the class.)

[I shrug my shoulders and furrow my brows.]

Cyrus – Are you alright now, Rinzee?

[I smile softly.] – Yeah...!

Skye[*teasingly*]– I think Jermey worked his magic on you with his charm...!

[*I blush.*] – No... no! it's not like that!

Cyrus[*teasingly*]– Rinzee, we know him...!

(Jermey gives a quick gesture to Skye and Cyrus, signaling them to stay silent.)

CHAPTER SIXTEEN

Growing Closer

(In Noah's class.)

Ryan – Noah, I want to ask you something.

Noah – Okay! Tell me?

Ryan – Austin told me that you and Daisy have been meeting daily in the park?

Noah – Yeah, so what?

Ryan – Do you have any idea that I like her?

Noah[*surprised*] – What? You never told me before! Wait...! Did you tell Daisy about your feelings?

Ryan – No...!

Noah – But why?

Ryan – Actually... I'm scared to tell her.

Noah – Then bro, that's your loss! I think she likes me too.

So, don't blame me later!

Ryan[*in a breaking voice*] – I'm not blaming you...! Yes, I lost my chance... and her too.

She's so beautiful. I wish... I wish I had the courage to tell her...

Please... please, Noah keeps her happy. Always be there to wipe her tears.

Noah – I understand your regret and concern. I promise you, I'll never hurt her, and I'll always keep her eyes shining.

(At Jermey's house.)

Jermey – Mom, please don't tell her about what I told you.

Kyler (Jermey's mom)*[playfully]* – Okay...! But should I tell her how much you talk about her? *[furrows her brows]*

Jermey*[blushing]* – No, Mom, please...!

Oh my God...! *[I placed my palms on my face and blinked.]*

(Then I rang the doorbell.)

(Jermey opens the door.)

[I nod appreciatively.] – Hello, Jermey...!

Jermey *[thinking, taking a deep breath and shrugging.]* – Oh, God...! So pretty...!

Hi... welcome, Rin!

Kyler*[grinning]* – Oh... my dear, Jermey is right. You're so beautiful.

[I nod appreciatively.]– Thank you... but Jermey is right about you too—you're so pretty.

Kyler – Come dear, meet Grayson, Jermey's dad.

Grayson – Hi, cham! How are you?

I – Hello, I'm fine! Ann... now I know why Jermey calls Noah cham.

Grayson*[laughs]*

(At the dinner table.)

Grayson – Tell me more about your family, Rinzee!

I – Well, I have my mum, my younger brother, Noah, and my dad, but my parents got divorced, so now he doesn't live with us.

Kyler – You know, Rinzee, Jermey used to write poetry when he was younger, but he hides it because he thinks it's embarrassing.

[My eyes widen.] – Wait... what?! Jermey... you? Writing poetry?

Jermey *[looking at his plate, fiddling with his spoon.]* – Yeah...!

I– Come on, Jermey, you can tell me at least.

Jermey*[pressing his lips together.]* – Hmm...!

[I look at him, trying to make eye contact.] – By the way, I love poetry.

Kyler – Oh... nice! Then, Jermey, you should tell her one of them.

Grayson – Yeah, this time, we're not accepting any excuses.

Jermey*[taking a deep breath]* – Okay, let's first finish dinner, then I will!

Kyler – Aww... my cham! As you want.

I– I'm excited.

(At Noah's home.)

Isabelle – Where's Rinzee, Noah?

Noah *[excitedly]* – Mum, you won't believe where she is!

Isabelle*[confused]* – Where?

Noah *[seriously]* – She's at the bar with her friends.

Isabelle *[shocked]* – What...?!

Noah – Mmm...!

Isabelle*[angrily]* – Did she forget that I don't allow at her age?! And if she really wanted to go, she could have at least asked me!

Noah*[laughs]* – No... no... She's at Jermey's house for dinner.

Isabelle*[staring at Noah and throwing a cushion at him]* – Noah....!

Noah – Heehee...!

(At Jermey's house.)

I– I'm waiting for your poetry, Jermey.

Kyler*[excitedly]* – Me too!

Grayson – Come on, my son, don't keep the ladies waiting.

Jermey *[sighs, running a hand through his hair]* – Okay...! So, listen...!

[Jermey takes a deep breath and begins reciting his poem.]

"Find someone who notices your smiling eyes and laughing lips,

the one who sees your shine even in the darkest of nights.

Maybe the one who knows the exact moment you need them,

who cherishes the purity of your heart,

not just the appearance others admire.

Maybe the one who feels like a breeze, even in pain—

not perfect,

but with you, becomes perfect."

[Silence fills the room for a moment. I blink, staring at Jermey, my lips slightly parted in surprise.]

I– Wait... what?!

Kyler*[grinning]* – Aww... that was beautiful!

Grayson - Not bad, huh? Told you he had a hidden talent.

Jermey *[avoiding my gaze, tapping his fingers on the table]* – It's just... something I wrote a long time ago.

[I smile teasingly.] – Just something? Jermey, that was amazing! Who knew you were secretly a poet?

Jermey*[pressing his lips together, looking anywhere but at me]* – Yeah, yeah... whatever.

[I lean forward, resting my chin on my hand, studying him.]

I– So... who was it for?

Jermey *[choking on his drink]* – What?! No one!

Kyler*[laughing]* – Now that's a question I'd like to hear the answer to!

Grayson – Me too.

Jermey[*groaning, hiding his face*] – Can we please change the topic?

[I chuckle, watching his ears turn red. This is fun.]

(After some time, Jermey and I were walking through the streets.)

[I glance at Jermey, curiosity nudging at me.] – Can I ask you something, Jermey?

Jermey[*humming*] – Mmm...!

[I hesitate for a moment, then decide to ask anyway.] – Please don't mind, but that poetry you wrote... who was it for?

Jermey[*staring at the sky*] – Star...!

[I blink in surprise, staring at him.] – Who...?

Jermey[*shrugging*] – No one....!

[I narrow my eyes playfully.] – Is there any imaginary girl, then?

Jermey[*gazing at the moon and stars*] – Maybe, maybe not...!

[Jermey and I stare at each other, the silence stretching between us, filled with unspoken thoughts. Something about his words lingers in my mind, refusing to fade away.]

(Later, the same night.)

[Jermey is sitting at his study table, thinking about everything that happened today.]

Jermey[*thinking*]:

How will I tell you, Rinz....? I have a fear of abandonment.

People always leave after some time, I don't know how Cyrus and Skye are still with me. But... but... but... I have fear of losing them too.

[He sighs and chuckles softly.]

Jermey[*muttering*] – Look at me... I've started talking like you — but... but... but....!

He leans back, eyes on the ceiling.
Jermey[*thinking*]:
Ahh... why does this always get so heavy?
Why do I forget the beautiful things, too?

CHAPTER SEVENTEEN

Facing the Shadows

(Next day, at school.)

Mr. Daniel Foster – Class, I'm thinking of having a debate activity today.

The topic for today's debate is: *Hamen Shishp vs Giana Mijee*

[Even as I sit in class, my mind keeps replaying Jermey's words from last night.]

Mr. Daniel Foster – Rinzee, I hope your thoughts aren't still wandering in the stars. Let's bring them back to the debate!

[I blink, snapping out of my thoughts as everyone turns to look at me.]

[Great. Now I look like a daydreaming fool in front of the whole class.]

Mr. Daniel Foster – As you all already know, *Giana Mijee* is the ruler of Georgiana.

Rinzee, do you know about him and his great work?

I– Yeah... not much...!

Mr. Daniel Foster – Alright, I'll divide you into groups, then we'll begin.

(Skye, Jermey, Cyrus, and Natalie end up in the same group.)

(Max, Rinzee, and Hannah are placed together.)

(The students settle into their groups.).
I'm thinking....
Why am I not with Skye and the others?
Shit...! I don't know anything about this, and I don't even want to be with these people.
Damn, why do I always end up in situations like this?
God, please help me...!
I– Max, please help me...!

Max – Don't worry, I got you!

Natalie *[dramatically]* – See, Cyrus? I'm always with you...!

Wherever you go, I'll follow. It's just how destiny works with us.

Cyrus – Just shut up, Natalie...!

Mr. Daniel Foster – Now, let's begin.

(The debate continues.)

Hannah*[angrily]* – Rinzee, would you at least say a single word?

(Skye's group wins the debate.)

Hannah – Rinzee, why didn't you say anything?!

Cathrine*(Hannah's classmate and friend.)* – Yeah, if she had spoken, we definitely would've won!

(Jermey sees that Hannah is saying angrily to Rinzee.)
(He steps into it.)
(Jermey notices Hannah yelling at Rinzee. He steps in.)

Jermey – Chill, guys! It's just a debate!

Hannah – You're only saying that because you won...!

Cathrine – But, why didn't she say anything?

Jermey – Do you not realize it's only been four months since she moved here?

Cyrus – Jermey, why are you even talking to these idiots?!

Just leave them! Let's go!

(Jermey grabs my hand.)
Jermey – Don't worry, Rin...!
Skye*[teasingly]* – Girl, were you meditating?!
Jermey – Skye...?!
Skye*[grinning]* – I'm just kidding!
Jermey – Yeah, we know... but seriously, stop for now!
[eyeing Skye] Rinzee, why are you so silent?
[I just stare at Jermey, lost in thought.]
Jermey – Rinzee...?
Skye – Oh my God! Why is she not speaking?!
Jermey – Rinzee, are you okay? (He gently shakes my shoulder.)

[I snap out of it.] – Yeah...! What were you guys talking about?

Skye – Rinzee, you scared us!

Jermey – Rin, please! Don't overthink. It was just a debate!

[I shrug my shoulders and furrows my brows.] – I'm worried because I was a scholar in Rinny... but now look at me!

Back there, everybody knew – She's the one who will win.

Here, I couldn't even say a single word! I completely freaked out during the debate!

Skye – Don't worry, Rinzee! We've got you!

Jermey – Yeah! With us by your side, you'll definitely do great!

I– Thank you so much, guys!
(The school day ends.)
Jermey – Come on, Rin, I'll drop you, home.
I– Okay...!
(Jermey and I get into his car.)
(I glance at Jeremy, lost in thought.)

I'm thinking....

Jermey is such a nice person. The way he handles everything so calmly...

I think... I like him...!

But do I really know him that well yet?

What if I tell him there's a spark in between us?

Does he feel the same way?

(Jermey notices Rinzee staring at him.)

Jermey[*thinking*]: *Does she feel the same way I do?*

Should I say something to break this awkward silence?

Jermey – Rinzee, have you tried the famous cookies from Georgiana's Snowy Crumble café?

I – No, not yet!

Jermey – What?! It's been four months since you moved here, and you still haven't tried them?!

[I feel a little shy and awkward.] – No...!

Jermey – Okay, then! Let's go!

CHAPTER EIGHTEEN

New Promises

(At Henry's home.)

Henry – I've been wanting to say something to you for a long time, Issaaa...!

Isabelle – Yeah, tell me...?

Henry[*nervously, getting on his knees*] – I really like you, Issaaa! I know it might be difficult for you to date someone just after your divorce...

But, please... give me a chance...! I promise, I'll never break your trust.

And most importantly... I'd be more than happy to be a father of two beautiful kiddos...!

Isabelle [*smiling softly*] – Henry... You're so sweet...!

Yeah, I'm ready to give it a try...! But... for now, give me some more time to think about this proposal.

I need some time...

I know you'll be a great dad... and an amazing husband too.

Henry – Take your time, Isaa! I'll wait for you.

[Both exchange a glance, then hug tightly.]

(At the Snowy Crumble café.)

Jermey – What cookies do you want to try?

Umm...! **[I think hard]**

Jermey – I'd say go for the coconut flavour—it's their specialty!

I– Okay, then let's order that... and Belgium chocolate chip cookies too!

Jermey*[grinning]* – Umm...! Nice choice!

I – Oh, I really like the coconut flavour!

Jermey – I'm glad you liked it!

I – Thank you so much, Jermey!

Jermey *[grinning]* – Oh, come on! You don't have to thank me for cookies!

Rin, tell me about your old school, your friends, boyfriends... and, of course, your beautiful city, Rinny!

I – Well, about Rinny – it's a beautiful city. And just like its name, it rains heavily most of the time. But honestly, I love it.

Jermey – Wow...!

[I smile softly.]– Hm...! And my school? I told you before—I was a scholar, so I always got attention from others. Even my principal wasn't happy about me moving here.

Jermey*[grinning]* – Oh wow...! That's impressive!

I – Oh God, my friends...! If you had asked me about them before, I would've been so happy to talk about them. But now? I think they've ghosted me... they don't even read my messages anymore.

I had two best friends – Tera and Kam. But ever since I moved here, Kam hasn't even called me once!

And Tera only called me once!

Tell me, is that how friends act?

Jermey – Yeah, you're right!

They have pretended so nicely to be your friends.

But, it's okay, Rinz....

That's life – people come and go.

Jermey[*thinking*]: *Wow... Jermey, you're saying this? Like, why does everybody have to feel this way? Should I tell her about my fear?*

She's gone through the same... so maybe she'll understand?

No... no... just stop!

Jermey – But I'll give you assurance - I'll always be there for you.

Maybe sometimes, it'll take me time to come, but I'll be there. That's my promise to you.

[I beam.] – Thank you so much, Jermey! It really means a lot.

Jermey – Don't be! *[grinning, teasingly]* – Rin from Rinny...!

[My cheeks warm.]

Jermey – Let's go! Rin.... Rin...!

[I cheekily reply.] – Okay! Jer... Jer! Mey... Mey!

Jermey[*laughs loudly.*]

(Jermey drops me home.)

Jermey – Here you go!

[I nod appreciatively.] – Thank you so much for everything, Jermey!

Jermey *[teasingly]* – Can you show me the stock of thank yous in your house? I think, I'll pick some!

[I laugh loudly.]

Sorry...!

Jermey – Oh, so you have a stock of 'sorry' too?

[I grin.] – No...!

Jermey – Bye, Trin... Trin...!

I – Bye, Jer... Jer...!

(At Giana beach.)

(*Isabelle walks along the beach.*)

Isabelle[*thinking*]: *I have faced a lot in my life. My past marriage was tough because my husband wanted us to see the* *world through his eyes.*

[looking at the sky...]

I don't want my kiddos to see the world through my eyes—I want them to make their own decisions. I can guide them, but I can't force them to live the life I want for them.

[looks at the flowing water... maybe just like this...]

After my divorce, I wished for someone to understand me too. But... I'll always wonder—will my kiddos accept my decision?

[blinks, places her right hand on left shoulder, and furrows her brows.]

I came here. I met Henry... he loves me. [blushing] and I love him too. But is love enough? Will my kiddos accept him? Will they accept us?

I know he'll be a good father—better than the one they had. He understands me in ways no one ever has.

Umm... I should give him a chance. Maybe this time, we'll finally be a perfect family.

[Isabelle takes a deep breath.]

I'll call him home tonight to tell him I've accepted his proposal.

CHAPTER NINETEEN

Secret or a Secret Promise

(At home, in my room.)

(In My home, in my room.)

(I lie on my bed, thinking about Jermey.)

Jermey is such a nice person... There's definitely a spark between us...

(Phone notification.)

(I grab my phone to check.)

What...?!

Why is Joe sending me a message saying –

I miss you, ZEE...

Should I tell my past to Jermey?

Everyone thinks I've never dated anybody...

But that's not true!

[I feel my chest tighten as I hold back tears.]

[in a broken voice] – I dated Joe for eleven months.

How can I tell everyone that I was a fool to love him?

That I trusted him blindly... and he betrayed me?

I grab my diary and let my emotions spill onto the page.

"Maybe I'm the person who is hard to be loved.

Hard; hmm, the one who knows but remains silent without making the situation violent.

Maybe I'm the person who is inhuman in the eyes of the devil of my life.

Inhuman; hmm, the one who says they don't know about the humanity I served to them.

Maybe I'm the person who is ruining the moment.

Moments; hmm, the one who doesn't become apathetic and forget all the moments I have created for them.

Maybe I'm the person who is ghosted by my special persons.

Ghosted; hmm, the one who makes special those who are ghosted by others.

Maybe I'm the person who remains quiet.

Quiet; hmm, the one who has shared some secrets once, yet they are known by everyone."

Just one month before our one-year anniversary, he cheated on me...

Double-dated me with someone else.

[I close my diary, holding it tightly against my chest. My breath trembles, and my fingers grip the cover. My past feels heavy, but I can't let it pull me down.]

(Just then, Isabelle calls me and Noah for dinner. I blink away my tears, take a deep breath, and get up.)

(At the dining table.)

Isabelle – Rinzee, why you look so worried?

Noah – Did Jermey say something to you?

I – No, nobody has done anything to me?

Isabelle – Then what happened, my kiddo?

(I suddenly feel a lump in my throat... and before I know it—)

I break down into tears.

[Mum hugs me.]

Isabelle – Rin, don't cry, kiddo...!

Noah – Please don't cry, Rin.

Isabelle – First, tell me –what happened?

I – Mum, Joe messaged me...! He said, 'I miss you'.

Isabelle[*angrily*] – Why is he suddenly messaging you this?! And you haven't blocked him yet?!

Noah – Yeah, Rin! You told me you blocked him!

Isabelle – There is no need to reply to him.

[I say in a breaking voice.]–Mum, why does he affect me so much?

Isabelle – Rin, it affects you because you gave him the power to affects you.

Noah – Rin, you need to move on. He's a terrible person. He doesn't deserve you.

Isabelle – Yeah, Noah, you're right! Rin, find a new man. Leave your old memories in the past, where they belong.

Noah[*teasingly*] – Rin, what do you think about Jermey?

Isabelle – Is he dating someone?

I – No... He's not dating anyone.

Isabelle – Okay, I'm not saying you have to date him only. If you like someone else, go for it... But don't stop yourself from experiencing love again.

I – But what about Dad? Remember when I was dating Joe... he told me I shouldn't date at this age. He was right! Look where I am now... I'm feeling the same pain he once felt.

Isabelle – No, Rin, It's not like that!

You and your dad didn't suffer because you dated... you both suffered because you choose the wrong person to experience love with.

Noah – Mum is right, Rinzee. Just move on from that bullshit cheater.

[I grin.] – Think about Jermey, huh! He's prettyyy good lookinggg...!

[I say, playfully.]– NOAHHH! OMG SHUT UP!

Isabelle - Kiddo...! It's time to sleep now!

(I and Noah went to sleep.)
Isabelle[*thinking*]: *Oh, these kids...!*
(Doorbell rings.)
(Isabelle opens the door, and Henry Collins is standing there.)
Henry– Hey, honey!
Isabelle – Hi, henry! Please come in quietly. Though my kids are sleeping... but you never know!
Henry – Okay!
Isabelle – I called you here today to tell you, my decision.
Henry – Oh God...! I've been waiting for this day.
Please... please, say yes...!
Isabelle[*takes a deep breath*] – Henry... [*blushing*]You can be my love, bells of my heart.
Henry[*grinning*] – Oh... Isaa...! I love you so much!
[Henry hugs her tightly.]
Isabelle – I love you too!
(Isabelle and Henry sit in the living room, spending their spending their quality time together.)
(After some time, Noah comes downstairs for something.)
Noah – Who's he?
Isabelle[*in a scared voice*] – He's Henry Collins.
Noah[*in a surprised voice*] – Your boyfriend?
Isabelle[*in a shaky voice*] – To be honest... yeah!
Noah[*smiling softly*] – Wow... mum! I'm happy for you!
Isabelle [*surprised*] – Really?!
(Noah hugs her tightly.)
Noah – Yeah, mum! You have the right to live your life freely.
Yes, you're my mum... but you're human too. You deserve love and happiness!
(Noah kisses her on her cheek.)

(Isabelle's eyes well up with tears.)
Noah*[smiling softly]* – Oh, so Henry…!
I'm Noah, my mum's little kiddo…! So nice to meet you!
Henry*[smiling warmly]*– Hi, Noah…! You're just like how your mom described you…! Nice to meet you too!
Noah*[grinning]* - I just want one promise from you?!
Henry – Yeah, tell me?
Noah *[smiling softly]* – Always be there for her and keep her happy…! She deserves the best.
Henry*[smiling sincerely]* – I promise you, kiddo…! I'll never let her down.
(Noah and Henry exchange a heartfelt glance and smile.)
Isabelle – Thank you so much, my kiddo…!
Noah – Love you, mum!
Isabelle*[wiping her tears and then smiling.]* – Love you, more!
Henry – Yeah, thank you so much, Noah, for understanding us!
Noah *[grinning]* – Just… remember my promise!
Noah – Mum, does Rin have any idea about this?
Isabelle – No, not yet.
Noah – Don't tell her now. She's already been through so much.
Isabelle – Aww, my fifteen- year- old kiddo has become so mature.
[Turning to Henry, smiling] Look, Henry…!
Noah *[grinning]* – Oh, come on, mum!
[teasingly] – Now, I'm going. Sorry for disturbing you guys.
Isabelle *[smirking]* – Noahh…!
Noah – Okay… okay…. I'm going!
(Henry laughs.)
(Henry walks up hugs Isabelle from behind.)

Henry[*smiling softly*] – Your kiddos are really sweet, understanding and mature.

Isabelle[*smiling*] – Haha! Well, you haven't met Rin yet. I mean, she's sweet and understanding too but...

I think, she'll take time to understand this!

Henry – Don't worry, we'll make it too, honey!

Isabelle[*smile warmly*] – Yeah... I hope so!

CHAPTER TWENTY

A Party or Confession Room

(Next morning, at my home.)

Isabelle – Kiddo...! I have a meeting regarding my book, so I'll have to go to Rinny for two days. Will it be fine for you both?

Noah*[smirking]* – Yeah, it'll be more fun if you're not here.

Isabelle*[surprised but smiling]* – Noahh...!

[playfully] – Yeah, you're right, Noah!

Isabelle – Okay, have fun...! But do not disturb our neighbours, alright!

Noah – No promises!

I – Hahaha...!

(At the school.)

Noah – Hi, Daisy!

Daisy -Hello!

Noah – My mum is going out of town for two days, so... would you like to come over to my place?

Daisy – Umm... yeah, sure!

Noah *[excitedly]* – Okay then! We'll have so much fun!

Daisy*[smiling softly]* – Yes...! I'm sure we will.

[I say excitedly.]– Guys, guys, guys…! My mum is going out of town for two days, so… we can have a party!

Tell me, Cyrus and Jermey, what do you say? Paaarty….!

Skye*[excitedly]* – Wow… Rinzee, we'll have so much fun.

Cyrus and Jermey*[excitedly]* – Yeah, we can have a paaarty…!

Cyrus – I'll bring snacks and drinks.

I – Okay then, see you guys there! will meet!

(At my home.)

Noah – Rin, my friend, Daisy's coming today….

[I say teasingly.]– Ohhh, Noah… Daisyyy….!

Noah*[blushing]* – Okay… I've teased you before, so now it's your turn!

[suddenly tensed]– Wait, wait, wait….! oh my Goddd!

Noah – What happened?

I – Noah, I've invited my friends too… for the party!

Noah*[shocked]* – What the fuck!

I – Now, what can we do?

Noah – You guys are having a party, right? So… me and Daisy can stay in my room.

[I smirk.]– Hmm…!

Noah – What….?! Do you have another plan?

[I purse my lips.]– No…!

[I say.]– Okay then! But…!

Don't you dare come downstairs for anything. If you need something, call me first.

Noah – Done, deal!

I – Please help me with the decorations.

Noah – Why, I'm not even invited to the party, so why would I?!

(At Rinny.)

(At the café.)

Isabelle[*smile warmly*] – Thank you so much, Henry, for coming here with me.

Henry – No, darling, it's nothing.

Isabelle – I just hope the kiddos are fine there!

Henry – Don't worry, your kiddos are mature.

(Ethan sees Isabelle at the café.)

Ethan(*putting his hand on Isabelle's shoulder.*) – Hey, Isabelle!

Isabelle[*surprised*] – Hello...!

Isabelle [*thinking*]: *Oh God...! Why did I have to run into him?!*

And look who else is with me – Henry...!

Ugh... so what...?! Isabelle, you're a free bird now. You can fly with whoever you want to.

Just don't give a shit about this man – who's unfortunately my husband. [smirking]

Ethan – Did you come alone?

Isabelle – Yeah, actually, I came here for work.

[smirking and flexing]

Ethan, meet him – Henry, my boyfriend.

Ethan [*shocked*] – Isabelle...! It's just been three months since we got divorced, and look at you – you've got a boyfriend now!

Isabelle – So what! As you said, I don't belong to you anymore.

So, I can be with anyone I want to be.

Ethan[*angrily*] – Do my kids know about this?

Isabelle[*angrily*] – First of all, they're not just your kids. They're ours.

Henry[*firmly*] – Stop it, Ethan!

You can't talk to her like that. She's my girlfriend now.

Ethan[*furious*] – Oh really? And now you'll tell me how to talk to her?!

Isabelle *[frustrated]* – Just, cool down, Ethan!
Stop creating drama hare!
(At my house.)
(Noah comes downstairs.)
Noah – Hi, Skye! You're looking pretty.
Skye *[smiling warmly]* – Hello, Noah! Thank you so much!
Noah – So... Skye, you guys are having party today?!
Is your boyfriend coming tonight?
Skye – No...! Noah, I don't have a boyfriend.
Noah*[teasingly surprised]* – What...! Don't tell me that!
Skye *[smirking]* – Noah, why don't you tell me about your girlfriend?
Noah – Aann...! She's coming today. But... for now, she doesn't know that I'm planning to propose her today.
Skye*[surprised]* – Really?
She's lucky! You've got a great sense of humour.
Noah*[flexing]* – Aahh...! I know that!
I have a feeling you might meet the love of your life today.
Skye *[smirking]* – What rubbish?
Noah – Trust me, my intuitions are always right.
I – Yeah, Skye, Noah's instincts are pretty strong.
[I say sarcastically.] – Are you both done with your nonsense? Or should I leave the decorations to the great love prophets?
Syke – Oh, come on, Rinzee!
(Doorbell rings.)
(Noah opens the door. Cyrus is standing there.)
Noah – Hi, bro...!
Cyrus – Oh, hey, Noah! Finally meeting you!
Noah*[smiling softly]* – Yeah!
Cyrus – Skye told me your friend's coming tonight?

Skye – My mistake, actually... she is his *girlfriend*.

Cyrus[*teasingly*] – Ooo...! Girlfriend at this age? Wow... pretty cool.

Noah – Yeah... it sounds cool.

(Doorbell rings again.)

(I open the door. Jermey and Skye are standing there.)

I – Hello!

Daisy – Hi!

Jermey – Hey, beautiful...!

[I blush.]

Noah – Hey, Daisy!

(Jermey whispers in Noah's ear.)

Jermey – Nice choice, bro...!

[Noah blushes.]

Noah – Thanks!

Cyrus – So... you're the one we've been waiting for!

(Daisy looks confused.)

I – Now it's time to go upstairs, Noah!

Noah [*pressing his lips together.*] – Yeah...!

Noah – Come on, Daisy. My sister's ahh...!

(They head upstairs.)

Skye – So, what's the plan?

Max – Hey, guys!

(I, Jermey, Cyrus and Skye all turn, surprised.)

Natalie – Baby, you're attending a party without me?!

Hannah – Skye, you didn't tell me there was a party?! You know how much I love them.

Eliza Thornton (classmate) – Hey, Rinzee, guess what? I'll record your party and put it on my YouTube channel.

[I roll my eyes.] – You'll get followers too.

[I blink in disbelief.] – Is this my house or a nightclub?!

Ryder Vaughn – Yo, what's up? This is a party, right?

[He smirks.]

Ryder – Don't worry, I'll *make* it one.

[I frown, confused]– What's happening?!

Jermey – Rin, just breathe. Stay calm!

Cyrus – Okay... my bad. I thought you invited everyone. So...!

Skye *[angrily]* – Are you kidding me?! I told you it was just **us!**

Cyrus – I swear, I didn't do it on purpose, Rinzee. I'm really sorry!

[I sigh.] – It just happened! It's okay!

[I laugh.] – What's done is done...

No more ifs or buts... just enjoy the paaartyyy!

Jermey*[staring at Rinzee, thinking]: Oh... this girl! How can someone not fall for her?*

Skye *[excitedly]* – Drinks, everyone?!

Noah*[pumped]* – Oh, yeah...!

(At Noah's room.)

Daisy – Noah, you have a nice room.

Noah*[thinking]:* Maybe you'll like me too.

Noah – Thanks!

Daisy*[surprised]* – Oh... you still have Hot Wheels?!

Noah *[smiling softly]* – Yeah... I like them a lot.

Noah – Daisy, there's something I want to tell you.

Daisy – Yes...!

(He looks into her eyes, feeling a little nervous.)

Noah – Daisy, I really like you. I know it's only been ten months since we met, and it might seem early...

(Noah gently takes Daisy's hand in his.)

But I want you to brighten my life with your beautiful petals– just like the daisy flower does.

(Daisy blushes and takes a deep breath.)

Daisy – Noah, I really like you too, and I want to be with you... but I think we're too young to fully understand this beautiful oscillation of hearts.

(*Noah presses his lips together, looking a little disappointed.*

Daisy smiles softly.)

Daisy – But... I want to feel it, understand it, before it's too late.

(*Noah's face lights up with a smile.*)

Noah – I get what you mean. So... let's figure out this beautiful oscillation together.

Daisy[*smiling*] – Yeah...!

Noah [*grinning, excitedly*] – Okay, guess what?! Tomorrow, I'll be walking into school as *Daisy's boyfriend.* Wow....!

[*He smirks.*] – My imagination is finally turning into reality.

[*Daisy laughs.*]

(At the Rinny...)

Henry – Isabelle, what you have done?!

Isabelle[*grinning*] – Oh, I did it!

[*She bursts into laughter, while Henry stares at her in surprise.*]

Isabelle – Henry, you won't believe it – even I can't believe it.

[*She laughs again.*] – Ohhooo....! I just announced to the world that you're mine!

[*Henry laughs too.*]

[*Henry takes her hand in his and kisses it softly.*]

Henry – I love you, Issaaa...! You're truly amazing.

Isabelle[*pressing her lips together, smiling.*] – I love you too, baby...!

(At my home.)

Hannah[*sarcastically*] – Are you sure, Rinzee, that you didn't organize this party just for any attention?

Jermey*[frustrated]* – What's your problem, Hannah?

Max – Just shut up, Hannah...! Don't create scene – you're standing in her house.

Hannah *[angrily, sarcastically]* – Oh, so you're telling me to shut up?!

Max *[sarcastically]* – Yeah... I am. Since everyone here now knows my secret – thanks to you.

And honestly? I'm happy you did it. Because I've finally accepted my truth, my beauty.

I'm gay, and I'm proud of it.

Hannah*[frustrated]* – Oh really?!

Jermey – Hannah, stop it now!

I– Hannah, honestly, I think you create these kinds of scenes just to get attention.

Hannah*[angrily]* – I'm done with you guys. There was a time when you were my gems. And look at us now...

Max – All of this happened because of you, Hannah. You're the one who spilled my biggest secret. So how can we trust you?!

Jermey – You're the one who filled Natalie's mind against Cyrus!

Hannah – I did it because I fell for Cyrus!

[Max and Jermey, shocked.] – What...?!

Hannah*[crying]* – Yeah, I liked him so much... so I did that. I thought maybe by doing that, he'd finally notice me.

But... he never looked at me like that way.

And about your secret, Max, I blurted it out by mistake.

But you know what? I told it to Jace... and he really likes you.

Max *[stunned]* – What...?!

Jermey – Hannah, stop making up stories!

Hannah – Trust me, guys, this time I'm telling the truth. *I'm thinking....*

Oh god, who's Jace now?

Why do these secrets always come out in my house?!

Max – How can I believe you now?

Hannah *[crying]* – Please believe me, guys...!

Jermey – If I believe you, then why didn't Jace tell Max himself?

Hannah – Because I told him Max wouldn't want anyone to know about his secret. And Jace... he's not ready either.

Jermey – Not ready?

Hannah – He's scared... scared to say it out loud. To accept it in front of everyone.

Max – Then, why did he tell you?

Hannah – I found out by accident... and he trusted me not to tell anyone. But I thought Mx deserved to know the truth.

I – Guys, I think we should believe her this time.

Jermey – Okay... let's see.

If you're playing us again, Hannah... then you're done.

Hannah – Okay ...!

(Meanwhile, in another room at my house...)

Eliza – Woah, Woah, Woah.... Something really interesting is going down here.

Let me record this- it's too good to miss.

Ryder – Dude, I thought I was the one who drank the most tonight.

Haahaa... turns out, I was wrong!

(In Noah's room.)

Noah – I don't think there are just four people downstairs anymore.

Daisy – Yeah... you're right. It's way too loud.

Noah – Should I go check?

Daisy – Maybe ask Rinzee first!

Noah – Umm... okay!

(Noah calls Rinzee, but I don't pick up.)

I – No, no, no...! Is this even my house anymore?!

What the hell have you done, Ryder?! You've turned it into a freaking bar!

Ryder[*completely drunk*] – Hey... Rinzee!

I'm thinking...

Oh God...!

Cyrus [*completely drunk*] – Rinzee, where's Skye?

Cyrus [*louder*] – Natalie cheated me. Oh, why am I even saying that shitty name?!

Jermey – Cyrus, stop it, bro...!

Skye – What's going on here?

I – Ahh... you're here!

Jermey – Ryder, do you even realize what you've done?

Ryder – What?! I'm not responsible for this. He should know his limits!

Skye – Jermey, stop wasting your breath on this guy.

I – But... where were you when all this was happening?

Skye – I was with the Jace.

I – Jace....?!

Skye[*whispers in my ear*] – I have some exciting news to tell.

Cyrus – Skye, come here.

(Cyrus grabs her hand.)

Cyrus – You were right. Yes, you were right... I have feelings for you.

I was foolish – I couldn't even realise my own feelings! I choose the wrong person to date.

(Everyone at the party starts whispering, surprised.)

Jermey – Well, looks like he's finally on the right track.

Cyrus – I only realised this beautiful feeling when you were the one helping me through my breakup.

Skye*[surprised]* – Cyrus, I think you're completely drunk.

Natalie – Yes, baby, Skye is right!

Cyrus – No, no... It's not like that!

Skye – I'm going back!

[I'm surprised] – What? But... why?

Skye – I just want to go home. Bye!

Jermey*[surprised]* – Skye...

Skye – Not this time, Jermey!

(Skye leaves for home.)

Ryder – What's wrong with her now?

Natalie – Cyrus will definitely regret this night.

Cyrus – Just shut the fuck up, Natalie! Are you blind and deaf?!

(Everyone in the party) – What the hell...?!

Ryder – Why does this girl always cheat? First, she cheated on Cyrus for me. Then she cheated on me to get him back.

Ryder – Wow... Natalie!

I'm thinking....

I can't take this anymore! Just shut up, everyone!

I – Please, please... stop it, guys.

Jermey – Yeah... just stop this. [sarcastically] Stop making this night even more amazing!

(After all the chaos, the party came to an end, and everyone left—except Jermey.)

[I sigh.] – What a crazy night!

Jermey*[laughs]* – Yeah...!

[I chuckle.]– Wow... so many secrets came out tonight, huh?!

Jermey – Yes... even Cyrus never told me!

But... I think, he'll definitely realize his mistake.

I – But, why did Skye act so wired? She likes him too.

Jermey – I think, she's not ready for this. It all happened so suddenly.

You know, Rin, Skye's very sensitive, emotional, and understanding.

She seems really cool—she is. I mean, she looks like she doesn't give a fuck about anything...

But deep down, she gives a fuck about everything.

I – Yeah... I think she hasn't even processed what happened today!

She'll take time to make her decision.

Jermey – Yeah... I just hope she makes the right one.

I – The right decision?! You mean she should accept the proposal?

Jermey – No! I mean whatever she feels is right, whatever is right for her.

[I look down, a soft smile tugging at my lips.] – Oh... Jermey, you're so understanding. You always think by analysing every side of a situation.

Jermey*[playfully shrugging]* – Come on, Rinzee! But Thanks!

I – What do you think about Jace's story?

Jermey – Umm... I think, Max should clear things up by asking him directly. Jace should be the one to tell him about his feelings.

I – Yeah... since Max has accepted his truth.

(Noah and Daisy comes downstairs.)

Noah – Is the party over already?! That was fast.

I – Don't even ask!

Noah – Why? what happened?

Daisy – Yeah... we heard so much noise.

Noah – And I called you so many times, but you didn't pick up.

(I and Jermey tell Noah and Daisy everything that happened at the party.)

Daisy *[surprised]* – Oh god...!

Noah – Why didn't you pick up my call, Rinzee? It sounded like so much fun!

[I say angrily.]– Noah... please!

Noah*[laughs]* – By the way, Cyrus is a lucky guy. Natalie dated him and now wants him back! Skye and Hannah both have feelings for him too.

Jermey*[laughs]* – Yeah, bro, you're right!

[I giggled.] – Guys... I never thought that my party would turn out like this.

Noah – Heehee....!

Daisy – Noah, it's too late now.

Jermey – Don't worry! I'll drop you off.

Rin, don't stress. Whatever happened, happened!

[I smile warmly.] – Yeah...!

Jermey *[in a sing song voice]* – Bye, Trin... Trin...!

[I feel my cheeks warm.]

[I mimic him with a smirk.] – Bye, Jer... Jer... Mey...!

Noah *[snickering]* – Aa... aa... ann...!

(At my room. I'm lying on my bed.)

I'm thinking, chuckle to myself softly.]

Today, my house turned into a bar.

What a party?! Should I call it a party or a court?

So many secrets came out today.

But why did Skye leave all of a sudden? She likes Cyrus! And when he finally confessed his feelings, she left.

How cool was it when Max finally found out that someone has feelings for him.

Oh god, Hannah— I really don't like this girl. She has such a different personality.

Aann.... Jermey. Oh Jer... Jer... Mey... [I blush]

Every time he calls me Trin... Trin... I feel like magic is coming towards me.

Ahh...! I really don't know when this boy will find me as curious as he did when he wanted to know more about me?!

Oh, I forget to ask Noah about his proposal date!

(Next morning, at my home.)

Noah – Rinzee, come fast! Look, I've prepared breakfast for you.

(I come downstairs.)

I – Wow, Noah, Daisy is really lucky.

Noah[*blushing*]

I – Yesterday, I forget to ask you about your date. Did Daisy accept your proposal?

Noah – Yeah...!

[I beam.] – Oh wow...!

[I nudge him playfully.] – Noah Woodrock has a girlfriend now.

Noah [*blushing*] – Isn't it pretty?! Having someone who's yours... only yours.

[I smile softly.] – So pretty...!

CHAPTER TWENTY-ONE

Confessions Under the Open Sky

(At the park.)

Cyrus – Tell me, bro, why did you call me here?

Jermey – Do you even remember single thing from last night?

Cyrus – Actually, I remember up until the party got crashed.

Jermey – So you don't remember what you did last night?

Cyrus[*scared*] – Don't tell me... Did I create a scene?

Jermey – Seriously, Cyrus!

Cyrus – Why are you creating suspense?!

Jermey – Okay... Just keep your heart strong.
You were completely drunk yesterday... and you confessed, in front of everyone, that you have feelings for Skye.

Cyrus [*nervous and guilty*] – Oh god...! What have I done?!
How did Skye react? She must be so mad at me!
She's never going to talk to me again...

Jermey – I don't know, but after your confession, she left without saying a single word.

Cyrus – I know... she's not ready for this. She helped me so much after my breakup.

[in a sad voice]: Before, I couldn't forget Natalie – every time I talked about her. But... but Skye never said, "Please, Cyrus, don't take her name," or "Stop thinking about her." Even after everything Natalie did to me.

[crying]: She... she never expected anything from me. She always listened to me without ever wanting to hear her own name with love, not even once.

And even if I did say it, she never even noticed – because she never expected it from me.

Jermey, all it took was just falling in love one more time... to finally realize – Skye is my love.

Jermey – I truly believe you, Cyrus. I understand your feelings—just go, my boy. Say all this to Skye once again.

She'll definitely understand you. And we both know how much she loves you too.

Cyrus*[looking at the sky]* – I hope so... Skye.

Jermey – But we don't even know where she is!

Cyrus – I know. come with me

(Ethan calls Noah, but he doesn't pick up.)

Ethan*[angrily]* – Now, he's not picking up my calls either!

I should call Rinzee... but she won't pick up my call either. She hates me too.

I think I should go to Georgiana and tell my kids about this.

(At school.)

Noah – Today, I'm entering school as Daisy's boyfriend.

Daisy *[blushing]* – And I'm entering as your girlfriend.

Noah *[grinning]* – Oh, this feeling.

Austin – Hi, guys! You both look cute together.

Celeste(Daisy's classmate and friend)[*smiling*] – Yeah, the most beautiful couple in school.

Daisy[*blushing*] – Thanks!

Austin[*teasingly, in a whispering voice*] – Did you kiss her?

Noah – Not yet, bro!

(At Giana Beach.)

Jermey – Are you sure she's here, Skye?

Cyrus – Yeah, I'm damn sure!

Cyrus and Jermey[*shouting*] – Skye.... Skye....!

(*Cyrus finds her sitting along the shore.*)

(*He places his hand on her shoulder from behind.*)

Cyrus – Skye!

Skye – Hmm...!

(*Cyrus sits beside her.*)

Cyrus – Skye, I know what I did...

Skye – Do you know why you did what you did?!

Cyrus – This time, yeah!

Every word I said to you was true. I know I'm drunk, but my words are not.

Skye – Cyrus, how can I believe you?!

Everyone at the party knows that I like you the most. But... you choose Natalie to date.

Cyrus – Skye, Natalie was my past. You know what I went through when she cheated on me. You were the closest one to see me—to see my inner voice, my feelings.

And it made me realize my mistake—choosing to date Natalie.

I was... I was so wrong to make that decision.

[in a crying voice] – As everyone around me could see what I couldn't.

Skye – But... Cyrus, I don't have the strength anymore to reconsider a decision I've already seen fail.

Cyrus – Please... please, Skye, give me one chance. I promise... I promise you this time, I won't hurt you.

Jermey – Yeah, Skye, this time, I can vouch for him.

If he'll break your heart then I'll break our friendship.

As you already know—everybody knows—you've been my favourite since childhood.

Skye *[in a confusing voice]* – But... Jermey...

Cyrus *[takes Skye's hand in his, takes a deep breath]* – *Skye, believe me... my heart wants your sky to fly like a bird.*

Trust me – I want to see every cloud change its shape according to your mood... or I should say, every season.

Jermey *[grinning, pressing his lips]* – Oh God!

Jermey – Skye, please say yes!

[Cyrus crosses his fingers.]

Cyrus*[kissing her hand]* – Skye, I want your clouds to rain their beautiful drops on my heart's land.

Jermey*[staring at Skye, gesturing her to say yes through his eyes.]* – Skye....

Skye*[blushing]* – Stop it, Cyrus, now!

Cyrus*[confused, shaking his head to the right]* – Skye, is that a yes...?

Skye*[blushing, staring into his eyes]* – Damn... Cyrus! Yeah, I'll allow my clouds to shine on your heart's land.

Cyrus *[hugging her tightly]* – I love you, Skye!

Skye – I love you too.

Jermey *[taking a deep breath]* – Finally...! I'm so happy for both of you.

Skye – Thanks! *[teasingly]* Jermey, you should tell your feelings to Rinzee too.

Jermey*[blushing]* – No... no...! It's not like that!

Cyrus*[teasingly, putting his hand on his shoulder]* – Bro, we know what you feel. After all, we are your best friends.

Skye – I think she likes you too.

Jermey[*pressing his lips*] – Hope so!

Jermey [*thinking*]: *What Skye said... is it correct?! What if she likes me too?*

[blushing] Wow... Damn...! The thought is making me happy. When this turns into reality.... OHH GOD....!

But... but.... but... [drawing something on the beach sand with his foot.] She's scared to love because of her father's past... because of what her father did when they caught us.

I think... I shouldn't tell her now...!

(At Rinny)

Isabelle[*narrowing her eyes*] – Henry, my intuitions are telling me that after knowing all this, Ethan won't stop here.

[in a shaking voice] He... he might do something big, something terrible. I know him.

Henry[*placing his hands on her shoulders and kissing her forehead.*] – Don't worry, Isaa! He won't do anything.

Isabelle – No... no... [*shaking her head*] Think Isabelle, think....!

I think we should go back home!

Henry – But why? The event isn't over yet!

Isabelle – No... I think we should go.

Henry – Okay... okay... just calm down!

CHAPTER TWENTY-TWO

Truths We Didn't Choose

(At the school.)

Max – Where are the others, Rinzee?

[I shrug.]– I don't know! Nobody came today without telling me!

(Ethan calls Rinzee.)

Ethan – Please... please! Pick up the call.

I'm thinking....

Why is dad calling me? Should I pick up his call?

Umm...! What if he's calling me to apologize?!

I – Yeah, Dad?

Ethan – My princess, where are you?

[I pause, surprised.]

I – I'm at school.

Ethan – Actually, I want to meet you. I'm in Georgiana right now.

I – Umm... Okay! I'm coming.

Ethan*[grinning, excitedly]* – Hey... my princess!

[I frown sightly, confused]– Hi, Dad!

I'm thinking...

What happened to him?! He's not angry with me now?!

Ethan – I want to tell you something. So, let's go home.

[Still unsure, but nodding] – Okay...!

(At home.)

Ethan – Listen to me carefully.

I – Hmm...!

Ethan – You already know about your mum and my relationship. But do you know about our love life?

[I'm baffled] – I'm not getting you!

Ethan – Oh...! so you don't know anything?!

[I'm perplexed]– Dad... I don't know anything. What are you talking about?

Ethan*[smirking]* – Your mum always had problems with me.

And now, she has a boyfriend.

[I'm completely bewildered] – What...?! No, I can't believe this. If she's dating, she would have surely told us.

She'll tell me everything. She knows I'll understand.

Ethan *[scoffing]*– You know your mum, she always wants to do things on her own, make decisions on her own without even discussing them with others.

She said that I force my decisions on others, but it's she who always does that.

I – No, Dad...! I mean...

Ethan*[scoffing]* – She did everything so fast. She said to me, "I have a boyfriend now."

I met her at Rinny. I met Henry too – your mum's boyfriend.

[I flinch in disbelief.] – "Dad, stop this now! I can't believe this."

Ethan – I'm just telling you the truth.

I think to myself...

Why... why Mum didn't tell me about this? [I scratch the floor with my toenail.]

Does she think I wouldn't understand her love, her relationship, her decisions?!

Am I that bad at understanding people?!

Why did she do this? If she had told me, I would have been so happy for her.

I've always respected her decisions. Wait a minute...! Did Noah know about this?!

Why does this always happen to me?! Why can't people trust me, believe me? Why am I talking about others when even my mum doesn't trust me?!

Ethan *[hugging her]* – My princess... don't think too much. I'm here for you.

[I force a smile, my voice laced with sarcasm.] – Hmm... yeah, I know!

Ethan – You should tell your mum that you won't accept this relationship.

I – But why?! Yes, I'm upset that she didn't tell me...

But I'm also happy for her—her new life, a new beginning, a new love that life is giving her.

She's our mum, but before that, she's a human—someone who deserves love, care, respect, and a beautiful touch.

You call me your princess, Dad, but this princess has seen something—there's a younger princess inside my mum too.

Ethan *[sadly]* – But... Rinzee you should understand my point too.

[I take a deep breath.] – Dad, I do understand your point.

I know, she was your love, and I know you still love her...

Ethan *[looking down, pressing his lips together.]* – Yeah, you're right. I do... I love her so much.

[I pause, thinking]:But... love isn't always enough, right? That's why you both... you know.

[I look away, struggling to find words]

I – It's not just about love. It's about understanding, about seeing things from each other's side. Maybe that's where things went wrong...

Ethan *[quietly]* – Your mum never saw my side.

[Taking a deep breath, I furrow my brows.] – Why do I keep thinking he'll understand...?

(On the way to Georgiana from Rinny.)

(In the car.)

Isabelle*[with a heavy heart]* – Why... why didn't I tell Rinzee about this?

Henry – No Isabelle, it's not that! At that time, we thought this was the right thing to do!

Isabelle *[crying]* – But if I had told her earlier, this situation wouldn't have happened.

My Rin... she might hate me for this.

Henry – Wait... wait... What did you just say? Might! so there's a possibility that she won't.

[Isabelle stares at him, blinking, then takes a deep breath.]

She'll understand what's between us. What will become between me and the kiddos.

Isabelle – But...

Henry – Isaa... We thought Noah wouldn't understand either, but he did. So why not Rin?

My heart says she will.

Isabelle*[pressing her lips together]* – I hope so...

(At school)

(Max is walking down the corridor, lost in thought.)

Max*[thinking]*: Should I talk to Jace about what Skye and Hannah told me?

(He keeps walking, distracted, until—)

Jermey – Hey, Max!

Max – Oh, hey! Where were you guys?

(He suddenly stops, eyes widening as he sees something unexpected.)

Max *[shocked]* – Wait…. Wait… Wait… Am I seeing this right?!

(Skye and Cyrus are holding hands!)

Max - OHHH MY GODD….! Umm….

(Skye and Cyrus exchange a glance.)

Max – You two look adorable together!

Jermey *[sarcastically]* – Well… not everyone is going to be a fan of this beautiful change.

[Cyrus suddenly notices Natalie and Hannah walking towards them, their expressions a mix of confusion and shock.]

[Without a second thought Cyrus pulls Syke close by the waist and…]

Cyrus *[looking into her eyes]* – May I?

(Skye brinks.)

[He kisses her—his eyes subtly watching Natalie's reaction.]

Jermey*[grinning]* – DAMMN….

Max – Woah! What a move, Cyrus! Yes…!

Natalie *[shocked, angry]* – Cyrus…?!

Cyrus*[sarcastically]* – Yes… Natalie?

Natalie – What did you do this?

Cyrus*[smirking]* – Can't you see?

Hannah – Natalie, there's no point in talking to him now.

Skye – For once in your life, you actually said something right.

Hannah – I always knew Cyrus loved you, I never understood why he choose to date Natalie.

[Jermey, Cyrus, Skye, and Max stare at her in shock. What's gotten into her now?]

Natalie *[eyes widening, voice barely above a whisper]* – What are you saying?

Hannah – Yeah… it's true! Don't forget, there was a time when Cyrus and I were really close. We're just friends now, but that bond was different. I know him better than anyone.

Natalie *[her voice unsteady]* – Now, even you're not on my side?

Hannah*[holding her gaze, voice firm but gentle]*– Natalie, it's not about sides. Sometimes, what truly matters is understanding the situation and choosing the right path—the genuinely right one.

[She looks at Natalie with sincerity.] – Just think about what I've said.

Jermey *[parting his lips in surprise]* – Woah… Woah… Woah… what a change, Hannah!

Max *[eyes widening, exchanging glances with Jermey]* – Yeah…!

Hannah*[shrugging, exhaling sharply, locking eyes with Natalie]* – I've always known what I need to do. *[Furrowing her brows]* – And I'm confident enough to accept my mistakes, my decisions and the lessons they bring.

Skye *[shaking her head, furrows her brows]* – She's always so damn cool.

Cyrus *[smirking]* – Yeah… I know her.

[In a louder voice, throwing his arms up] – So, Hannah is BACK, EVERYBODY!

Hannah *[grinning]* – By the way, congratulations, Skye. You got this!

Skye *[blinking in surprise, then smiling]* – Thank you… for understanding us.

Cyrus *[chuckles, shaking his head]* – Man, things just got interesting.

Jermey*[glancing around]* – Max, where's Rinzee?

Skye – Yeah, where is she? She'd be so happy to see us like this.

Max – Her dad came to pick her up, so she left with him.

Jermey*[eyes widening]* – What...? Her dad! Oh God... not again!

Cyrus*[raising an eyebrow]* – What's going on?

Jermey *[running a hand through his hair]* – Nothing, dude. I'll catch up with you guys later.

[Jermey suddenly spots Noah at the playground.]

Jermey*[raising his voice]* – Noah...!

Noah *[walking toward him, frowning]* – Yeah... what happened? Why do you look so worried?

Jermey *[furrowing his brows, narrowing his eyes]* – Did you know your dad was here?

Noah*[stopping in his tracks, eyes widening]* – What? When?

Jermey – This afternoon. And guess what?! He took Rin with him. *[press his lips together.]*

Noah *[stunned]* – What...! I'm scared. What happened to him all of a sudden?

[Noah quickly pulls out his phone and calls his mum.]

Noah*[voice trembling]* – Hello, mum... Dad came here and took Rin somewhere.

Isabelle*[shocked]* – I knew it... I knew this would happen! Noah, listen carefully— your dad saw me with Henry.

Noah*[eyes widening]* – Damn...!

Isabelle – Yeah... he knows about us. And he's definitely going to tell Rinzee.

[Noah clenches his jaw, running a hand through his hair.]

Isabelle – Just find him and handle the situation for now. We're on our way home.

Noah – Okay, I'll handle it!

Noah – Jermey, I think dad will go home. He won't hurt her. I know he's not a good father or husband, but he's not a bad person either.

Jermey – Alright then, let's go!

(Jermey and Noah exchange a glance before hurrying to the car, their steps quick and restless as they head home.)

Jace – Are you guys dating now?

Skye – Yeah...

Max – Yes, they are!

Jace*[excitedly]* – Wow! That's amazing. I'm so happy for you both!

(In the Jermey's car.)

Noah*[tense voice]* – I'm really worried about her. She can't take all this.

Jermey – We're going, we'll find her. Don't so worry so much—she's a strong girl.

Noah *[rubs his forehead]* – Yeah... that's the problem. She looks strong, but emotionally... she's not.

Did you know about her past relationship trauma?

Jermey*[surprised]* – What...?

Noah – Rin had a boyfriend. Or I should say... a monster.

Jermey*[shocked]* – What? She dated someone?

Noah*[rubbing his eyes with both hands.]* – Yeah. She dated him for eleven months. And he... cheated on her. Double dating.

Jermey – How can someone cheat on such a sweet, kind girl?!

Noah – She's already dealing with so much. And our dad—Oh God... that man!

[Moves his hands in frustration]

You know what happened that night... when you and Rin were –

Jermey – Yeah... yeah. Oh God... why always her?

[He furrows his brow, a soft sadness in his eyes.]

She's so sweet, so cute, so understanding. How can someone hurt her like this?

(Meanwhile, at school)

Cyrus – I think we should also go help Jermey.

Skye – Yeah, you're right. But we don't even know what's going on.

Jace – Actually, I know a little about it.

Cyrus[*surprised*] – Wait, what? Tell us!

Jace – One day, I overheard Jermey and Rinzee talking about her dad and his past love life. I wasn't trying to eavesdrop — I just happened to catch some of it while passing by.

But that's all I know—I didn't really pay attention to the rest.

Cyrus – Come on, let's go to Rinzee's home!

(At my home.)

(Jermey and Noah arrive.)

Noah [*nervously*] – Rin...

As soon as I saw him, I hugged him tightly, my eyes filled with tears.

Jermey stood silently, his eyes full of care and kindness as he looked at me.

Noah [*his voice slightly shaky, eyes glistening*] – What happened Rin?

Did Dad say something to you?

I'm thinking....

I'm not nervous to tell him about Mum's love life.

Nahh... I'm nervous because I have to tell him something she couldn't say herself.

I – Noah... you know, Mum has a boyfriend now.

[He presses his lips and rubs his forehead, not saying anything.]

[Tears roll down my cheeks.]

Why... why... couldn't she tell us?

[I glance at Jermey.]

[He doesn't say anything, just looks at me quietly.

But in that silence. I know something's stirring in him.]

Jermey*[thoughts]:*

Why does she always have to carry so much pain?

Why does she always hold on to this feeling— this abondance of trust?

I *[frowning, confused]* – Does she think we won't understand her?

Noah – It's not like that! I mean, I know what thoughts you're having right now.

But... Rin, she didn't tell you because you're already going through so much—Joe, your past...

[My forehead furrows and I blink in surprise] – Wait... wait... wait... What did you just say?

She *wouldn't* tell me?

[My lips part, and my eyes fill with tears] –

That means... you already knew, didn't you?

Jermey*[thoughts]: I can't see her like this anymore.*

Noah*[shrugging, his eyes glistening, voice barely a whisper]* – Yeah...

(Isabelle and Henry arrive home.)

Isabelle *[eyes filled with tears, lips parted, places her hands over her mouth]* – Aww... my Rin...!

[My first thought was to hug her tightly but then...]

[I say in an angrily voice.] – Don't talk to me, Mum!

If you can't trust me... You think Noah is more understanding than me?

If you had told me, I would've been so happy for you.
Even now... I'm still happy for you. But...
[My tears roll down my cheeks, my voice breaking.] – Why didn't you tell me?
I never imagined that this beautiful news... I'd hear it from Dad, and in this way.
Isabelle *[tears brimming in her eyes, forehead furrowed, in a weeping voice]* – Oh... my kiddo... Rin...
(Cyrus, Max, Jace and Skye arrive.)
Cyrus[*hurriedly]* – Are you guys alright?
Everyone looks surprised.
[Jermey gestured for them to stay quiet, placing a finger on his lips.]
[My voice trembles, eyes wide with disbelief.] – No... no... Mum... please...
[I got lost, staring at the floor.]
Skye[*in a shaking voice]* – Rin...
[I hold back my tears, then suddenly grab Jermey's hand and walk out of the house.]
Noah – Rin, where are you going?
Jermey – Don't worry, I'm with her.
(Jermey and I sit in Jermey's car.)
Jermey[*in a scared and confused voice]* – But where are we supposed to go?
I *[weeping softly]* – Anywhere... just drive. Please, just take me away from here.
Inside the house –
[Isabelle paces in distress, tears in her eyes.]
Isabelle – Shit... shit... shit... what just happened?! It's my fault. She's hurting because of me.
[Henry steps closer, gently takes her hand.]
Henry – No, Isaa... we're both responsible. And I you–I'll bring her back.

In the car –

I rest my head against the window, staring outside. My vision blurs with emotion as thoughts swirl in my mind:

Why... why would she do this to me? Am I really that hard to understand?

Why is it always the people I love who end up hurting me the most?

"Mum, you promised to stay. You drew the lines of my palm, but those lines...they don't seem to hold us together. Maybe... maybe not?

You promised to always have me. You created the sense of my unfiltered senses. The sense of you helped me meet my own.

Maybe, maybe not?"

Jermey[*thoughts*]:

Oh... my Rin... I don't know how to tell you this, but your tears feel like an ocean — pulling your eyes in like a sinking ship.

I can't even begin to understand the pain you're carrying... But what I can give you is a promise — that I'll never be the reason you feel like this. Never... never.

I have the fear of abandonment, but I don't want you to ever face that fear. Please... please no...

[All is silent in the car. Jermey is giving me my space, letting my emotions rotate around my heart and revolve through my mind.]

Inside the house –

Noah – Guys, do you have any idea where they might've gone?

Cyrus – Honestly... no.

Skye[*hurriedly*] – Yeah, I know! Jermey must've taken her to Giana Beach. But I think, for now, we should leave them alone.

Trust me Noah — Jermey will take care of her. He really will.

[Skye rolls her eyes with a little smile.]

He's going to kill me for this... but sorry, Jermey. I have to say it now.

[She takes a deep breath.]

Jermey loves Rinzee. So much.

Noah *[grinning]* – I knew it... I knew it. I'm so happy for her.

Yay....! Finally, my girl found a right person for her.

Isabelle *[wiping her tears]* – Wow... Jermey will be right for her. Even I'm so happy for her.

(Ethan arrives from the market, carrying food for Rinzee.

He stops in surprise seeing everyone there.)

Isabelle[*sarcastically*] – Welcome, Ethan! Surprised? Oh, no... no... you must be shocked to see me here, right?!

Isabelle[*angrily*] – I never imagined you'd stoop to this... shit, Ethan!

Ethan[*in a shocked and shaky voice*] – I... I...

Noah[*with a sarcastic smile*] – You used to call Rin a princess, didn't you? Wow... what a "princess" treatment you've given to her!

(Cyrus, Max, Skye, and Jace remain silent.)

Ethan *[shrugging, moving his hands.]* – I just told her the truth. Why is everyone acting like I caused all this?!

Isabelle[*forehead furrowed in disbelief*] – Do you even realise what you've done? Because of this... Rinzee has left. She's gone somewhere.

Ethan[*shocked*] – What...?

Henry – Yeah... and now, please, just leave us alone.

CHAPTER TWENTY-THREE

A Star Wants to Shine Again

(At Giana Beach.)

[The waves touched my feet—cold and soft—just like the ache inside my chest. My beautiful space full of stars. The sky above was fading into orange and pink, but inside me, everything was grey.]

(Jermey stands beside me, quietly. He's continuously staring at me.)

[Jermey's thoughts]: Should I speak now?

Jermey*[takes a deep breath.]* – Rin... please speak up now.

I know, you're going through so much... but please, forgive your mum for this.

I – But... but...

Jermey – Actually, Noah told me everything. About your past... your relationship trauma.

[I looked at him, surprised.] – What? When?

Jermey – When we were coming to your home to see you. Rin... don't worry. Everyone has a past. Different kinds of past.

The thing is what that make you to understand about yourself, about your life, about your growth.

[I looked into his eyes, thinking — how can someone be this understanding?]

Jermey – It's like... let the twinkle of your stars be so bright that no one notices your scars.

Me – Mmm...

Jermey*[holds my hand and looks into my eyes]* – Rin... I'm always with you. I'll never let you feel like this.

He looks at the flowing water – "I... no, Rin. Not this time.

[I got more curious...]

Jermey – Maybe... some other day. For now, let's go back to your home.

[I placed my palms on my cheeks.] – Not now....

(Suddenly, Henry arrived, slightly out of breath.)

Henry*[breathing heavily]* – Rinzee... please come back. Your mum, Noah, and I are really worried.

[I just stared at him. I didn't even know what I was thinking.]

Henry – Look, Rinzee... I know it might be hard for you to understand everything right now. But... it's just that you were already going through so much— that's the only reason we didn't tell you.

Me – But...

Henry*[shaking his head]* – I know... I get it. But trust me, I'd never let your family go through the pain your dad caused. Never.

[I lower my gaze, trying to steady my voice.] – You know... umm, my mum, Noah and I have always wanted a perfect family.

A perfect family isn't about everyone being perfect in their roles... it's about accepting each other's flaws, understanding each other's perspective, respecting each other's decisions—choosing us over anyone else.

[I smile with a blink.] – I know you'll play your character very well.

So…. Welcome, Henry….!

Henry smiled—wide and warm, like he finally felt better.

Jermey[*staring at them, smiling*] – Finally…!

Henry – Now, let's go home.

I – Yes, Ryy…

Henry[*looks at me in surprise*]

[My forehead furrows and my eyes smile.] – Yeah… Henry… Ryy…!

(At my home.)

Isabelle[*hugs me, tears in her eyes.*] – Oh, Rinzee…

Henry – Isaa, you know what? We won!

Noah[*smiling in surprise*] – Really? But I knew it… I know my Rin!

Isabelle – Thank you so much, Rin… I love you so much.

[Henry and Noah exchange a glance.]

Henry & Noah – We love us.

(Cyrus, Jermey, Skye, Jace, and Max stand nearby, eyes filled with quiet joy as they take it all in.)

(Later that evening, in the living room…)

(Isabelle picks up her phone and dials Ethan.)

Isabelle[*calmly, but firmly*] – Rinzee has come back home… she's fine now. *[glancing toward her]*

[pauses, takes a breath]

But Ethan… please don't come here right now.

I think she needs peace more than anything.

We'll talk… when the time is right.

(She hangs up, pressing the phone to her chest for a moment, her eyes closed.)

(At Jermey's room. The lights are dim. A small table lamp glows beside his bed as he lies there, staring at the moon through his window.)

[Jeremy keeps switching the lamp off and on, again and again.]

I'm Thinking...

It's so strange... how someone's presence and absence can affect you like this.

Like this lamp... either lighting you up or leaving you in the dark. Just like my fear of abandonment.

Dear moon... you know....

"I wanted her—

maybe she wanted me too.

She wanted me—

maybe she forgot that too.

I wanted to say something to her—

maybe she wanted that too.

She wanted to have me—

maybe she knows why it couldn't be.

I wanted to sit with her—

maybe she wants to take that step too.

She wanted to create us—

maybe she forgot how to.

I wanted to hold her—

maybe she did,

but forgot to reach out again."

Moon *– Jermey, that's really... really adorable.*

I know you want her. And somewhere... she wanted you too.

Please don't think she forget. And please

Remember—she held your hand when the room was full of her special, closed and loved ones.

Umm.... I think it's time now—for you to confess your feelings to her.

Jermey *– Really...?*

Moon *– Yeah, I think... it's the right time now.*

(Jermey falls asleep while staring and talking to the moon.)

(At Noah's home.)

(Noah is on a call with Daisy, telling her about everything that happened today.)

Noah – Daisy, I know Rinzee says she's fine... but I can tell—she's not. She won't say anything because of Mum's happiness. That's just how she is.

Daisy – Yeah... I understand.

Noah – It's not that she's not happy for Mum, but the way it happened...it was too sudden for her.

Daisy – Noah, give her some time. Let her heal in her own way.

Noah – But...

Daisy – Then talk to her. You know she'll listen to you.

Noah – Hmm... yeah.

(At my washroom, I'm looking into the mirror.)

I'm Thinking....

A ballon of secrets burst today. [I wipe my tears.]

I'm happy for Mum... she's found love again. Maybe this time, we'll get better Dad too.

For me... [I shrug my shoulder.] but... but... but today, I realised that Jermey is really important in my life.

He understands me so well... so deeply. Like he feels like music—somethingthat can sparkle my mood. [I blush.]

[That night, I couldn't sleep much. The sky outside my window was quiet, but inside me, a storm was slowly trying to settle. Maybe things are changing. For good.]

(Next day, at school)

Skye – Cyrus, did you talk to Rinzee after everything?

Cyrus – Nope, baby.

Max – I know things seem to be on the right track now... but still, I'm worried about her.

Skye*[pressing her lips]* – Me too.

Cyrus – But I really think Jermey will help her to heal. I'm super confident about that.

Jace – Yeah... Cyrus is right.

Jermey – Hey guys, what's up?

Cyrus – Hey! Did you talk to Rinzee later?

Jermey – No... actually, I thought I should give her some time—to think, to understand, and to heal.

(In the car.)

Noah*[in a guilty voice]* – Rin, I'm sorry I told Jermey about your past with Joe...

[I look at him.] – No, it's okay. I think... whatever happened or happens, maybe it's for the good of today and better for tomorrow.

Since I had to tell him anyway. Now he knows—great!

Noah – And I'm sorry for not telling you about Henry.

[I press my lips together.] – No... no, Noah. It just happened. I know you.

Noah *[gazing at her]* – I love you, Rin. I'll always be by your side—no matter what.

[I smile.] – Aww... I love you too.

(In the class...)

Skye – Hey, Rin... are you okay now?

Max *[furrowing his brows]* – Yeah, we were really worried about you.

[I smile softly.] – Yeah... I'm okay. And I'm happy too about everything that happened. I know it was all so sudden, but... *[I lift both hands gently, as if to show acceptance]* I'm happy.

Jace – That's nice! And guess what... we have amazing news for you.

[I raise a brow, surprised.] – What?! Not again!

Jace – First listen...

You know Cyrus proposed to Skye. *[I look at them.]* And Skye said yes...

[I say excitedly.] – What....?! Eeeeee! I'm so happy!

[I hug Skye tightly.] – Aww... I miss this. [I furrow my forehead and blink.]

Cyrus[teasingly] – I think we want that from you too.

[I stare at him, cheeks warming up.] – What do you mean?

Jermey[nudges me gently with his shoulder] – You really don't know what he's saying?!

Max – Seriously... Rin?!

[I look away.] - Yeah... I really don't know!

(The class continues...)

(Everyone starts focusing on their notes again, but my mind is still lost somewhere else.)

CHAPTER TWENTY-FOUR

A Night to Remember

(In the corridor.)

Principal Dawson[*clapping to get attention*] – Alright everyone! I have a little surprise for you all.

(Everyone goes quiet, turning toward him.)

Principal Dawson[*smiling*] – This Friday, we're organizing Georgiana High's Winter Formal!

It'll be held at *Giana Beach Pavilion* — yes, the beach!

[A few gasps and cheers echo around.]

Principal Dawson – It'll be a magical evening with music, dancing, fairy lights, and there is a rule that everyone has to come with someone, it might be a friend or you guys know.

Natalie[*Thinking*]: *With whom should I go?*

Principal Dawson – So, get ready, everyone—for a beautiful and fun evening!

Cyrus[*excitedly*] – It's goona be fun, baby...!

Skye[*smiling*] – Yeah....!

[Jermey and I exchange a glance. Like... we both want to ask each other to be our partner, but something just holds us back.]

Max[*glancing at Jace*] – Who am I even gonna go with?

[Jace fidgets, avoiding max's gaze.]

Jermey – What happened to you, Jace?

Hannah *[whispers in Max's ear]* – Ask Jace to go with you.

Max – Really...?! What if he says no?

Skye – Then at least you tried. And if he says yes, you both can show everyone that you're not scared of your truth anymore.

Hannah*[smiling at Skye]* – Yeah... she's right.

[I whisper in their ears.] – What are you guys talking about?

[Hannah, Max and Skye jump a little, surprised.]

Hannah – You scared us, Rinzee!

[I smile.]

Skye – Actually... we're trying to convince Max to ask to Jace to go with him to the Winter Formal.

I – Umm... that's actually a nice idea. You should totally try, Max.

Max – But Hannah, you told me that he's not ready to let others know about his reality.

Haanah – Yeah... but what if he feels more confident with you?

Skye – Just go, Max...!

I – Max, just be confident!

Cyrus – Do you have something planned, Jermey?

Jermey*[confused]* – What are you talking about?

Cyrus – Just don't make me feel like I'm being foolish. I know you and Rin like each other—so say it, man.

Jermey – Hmm... I want to. But you know very well how hard it is for her to find peace. There's so much going on in her life.

Cyrus – Yeah... you're right. But don't lose your chance.

Jermey – Hmm...

(At the Moonlight beach.)

Isabelle – What do you think about a family dinner?

Henry – Yeah... I'm ready for it. But you should ask Noah and Rin too.

Isabelle – Yeah... this time, I won't repeat that mistake again.

Henry[*in a nervous voice*] – Are they happy with me?

Isabelle[*looking at him*] – Of course they are. Don't worry.

[*She hugs him.*] – I love you so much. Please don't break my heart.

Henry [*kissing her forehead*] – I love you too, baby. I don't break what's mine.

(At night.)

Noah – Rin, are you going with Jermey at the Winter Formal?

Isabelle – What? Winter Formal?

Noah[*excitedly*] – Yeah... school is organizing it. And guess what? The venue is Giana Beach.

Isabelle – Wow... sounds really cool!

Noah – So Rin, tell us... who are you going with?
I'm thinking....
How do I tell them that no one's asked me yet?!

I – I don't know. Don't you guys have any other topic to talk about?

Isabelle – Well... I actually wanted to ask you something.

Noah and I – Yes, please!

Isabelle[*in a hopeful voice*] – I'm thinking to inviting Henry for a family dinner.

I – Yeah... please invite Ryy. We'll get to spend more time together.

Noah[*looking at me in surprise*] – Ryy... huh?! Nice!
[*I flick Noah's arm and smile.*] – Noahh...!

(Next day, at school.)

Max – Rin, do you know that Cyrus is going to ask Skye today for the Winter Formal?

[I looked at him, surprised and excited.] – Really?! Wow....

Jermey*[in a hurried voice]* – Guys, why are you here? Come on, we have to record Skye's reaction!

Max – Yeah, sure. Let's go.

Jermey*[looked at me, his eyes warm.]* – Oh... by the way, you're looking really pretty, Rinz....

[I nudged him, trying to act cool, even though my cheeks were totally warm.]

(At the playground.)

[Cyrus drops to one knee, holding out a bouquet of baby's breath and blue hydrangeas.]

[Skye's cheeks turn pink as she bounces with joy, her hand flying to her mouth in surprise.]

Cyrus – Baby, these blue hydrangeas remind me you— Skye. Soft, beautiful... just like your name.

And I want you to fly freely, like this beautiful baby's breath.

Will you please come with me to the Winter Formal... to cherish us?

Skye [smiling]– Aww... Cyrus!

Of course... yes!

[They kiss.]

[Everyone around pause, smiling—some whispering, "I want this too."]

Max – I think this is the cutest among all which are happening these days.

(Everyone starts whispering, "look there, Zayden is asking Natalie for the Winter Formal!")

Hannah*[sarcastically, crossing her arms]* – Looks like both of them were dying to ask someone. [sighs] Fine.

Jermey – At least she found someone. Otherwise, we'd have to survive the drama all over again.

[Max and I laugh.] – Yeah...

I – By the way, Hannah... who are you going with?

Hannah – Well, no one's asked me yet.

Max – Oh... Hannah, why didn't you ask someone?

Hannah - But I think I'll go alone and enjoy my own vibe.

I – That sounds cool too.

Jermey – Come on, guys. We have class.

(In the corridor...)

Noah*[calling out]* – Hey, Jermey!

Jermey – Hey, you're going to the Winter Formal with Daisy, right?

Noah*[sighs with a smile]* – Umm... yeah!

Noah – But I wanted to ask – why haven't you asked Rin yet?

Jermey *[pressing his lips together]* – I want to... but...

Noah – Just ask her, man. I'm damn sure she wants that too.

[Jermey smiles, rolling his eyes.]

(At my home.)

Isabelle – Why am I so nervous about the dinner? You guys have already met henry!

Noah*[hugging her]* – Mum, chill! It's just dinner... for a new, fresh—or should I say, beautiful—chapter.

[I admire them.] – Yeah... I'm damn sure Ryy will be lucky for our family.

His arrival has already brought us so much happiness.

Noah – Yeah... and finally, we can be a happy, sweet family.

[I press my lips together.] – But there's one problem...

Noah *[confused]* – What?

[I laugh.] – He's an investment banker.

Noah[*laughing*] – But he's a writer too!

[*Noah and I laugh even louder.*]

Isabelle[*teasingly*] – Kiddos...!

(At the Snowy Crumble café.)

Max[*in a whispering voice*] – Guys, should I ask Jace now?

Cyrus – Yeah... of course.

Max – Do you think he likes me?

Jermey[*smirking*] – Not think—he obviously likes you.

Max – Okay...

[*Max walks over, takes a deep breath.*]

Max – Jace, I know... we might be hard to understand for some people, but what really matters is that we understand each other.

Jace [*confused*] – Why are you saying this all of a sudden?

Max[*taking another breath*] – Umm... Will you come with me to the Winter Formal?

Jace[*in a guilty voice*] – Max, you're an amazing person. But... I don't think I'm ready to accept this in front of everyone at something as big as the Winter Formal.

[*Jermey and Cyrus glance at each other, clearly surprised.*]

Jace – I'm really sorry. It's not about you... it's me. I've been foolish, not strong enough to accept this part of me.

Max[*forcing a smile*] – No... no it's okay. It's your choice. No problem....

Jermey – What just happened?!

Cyrus – Why did we even push him into this? Max won't take it lightly...

Jermey – Yeah... I know.

Max – Guys, let's just go home.

Jermey[*hugging him*] – Please, don't be so hard on yourself, Max.

Just be...

Max – No... no, it's okay. I'll still come to the Winter Formal—just like Hannah said—I'll enjoy my own vibe.

Cyrus – Maybe the right one hasn't held the thread of your heart yet.

Max – Yeah... maybe.

(At my home.)

(The doorbell rings, and Isabelle opens the door.)

Isabelle[*smiling softly*] – Hey, welcome, Henry!

Henry[*smiling warmly, hugging her*] – Hey, baby!

I – Hey, Ryy...

Noah[*teasingly*] – Hey, Rin's Ryy!

[Henry laughs.]

[I flick Noah, smiling.]

Noah – Sorry, but I'm curious... what's in that?

Henry – I got you famous pudding from Giana's Apii Shop.

[Noah and I exchange a glance.]

Both – Impressive...!

Henry – Noah, I've heard you play the guitar?

Noah[*smirking*] – Oh... so what else do you know about us? Or should I say... Mum's kiddos?

Isabelle[*blushes softly.*]

Henry – Tonight, I'm not leaving without hearing you play.

Noah – Sure... but you'll have to listen to poem too. We have a poet in the house.

Henry[*surprised*] – Who? Rin?! Wow... Rin. Isaa never told me about this.

(After dinner.)

(The table is cleared, the lights are dimmer, and the cozy hum of quite laughter lingers in the air.)

Henry – So... with whom are you both going to the Winter Formal?

Isabelle*[feeling nostalgic]* – Oh... Winter Formal... those were the days!

Henry – Yeah... I know!

Noah – I'm going with Daisy.

Isabelle – What about you, Rin? Did Jermey ask you?

I – Well... not yet.

Henry – Why would you wait for him to ask?

[I stare at him in surprise.]

Henry – Yeah... I mean, it's not necessary that only boys should ask.

Maybe, he's just hesitating... knowing everything that's been going on in your life.

Isabelle – Yeah... maybe!

Henry – Okay... let Noah play the guitar for us.

Noah*[with a gentle happiness]* – Alright... then.

(Noah starts playing the guitar and singing softly.)

"I found a place near my heart...
But it's far away.
How I wish to come closer...
Maybe I'm the loser.

No wonder remains in my heart...
My eyes look so... so... dark.
I'm waiting for you...
To cherish our hearts.

The darkness of my eyes fades when you shine...
My baby... my heart will find.
My voice is not reaching you...
Maybe my message, my pain in silence, will find you.
My every wish becomes half...

As it wants the promise of you.

Let me find a place again...
Or meet me behind the garden of wrongs.
Vanish all the scars...
My baby... my meteors will find."

(And the song continues....)

(At Giana Beach. The night is quiet, but the gentle sound of waves fills the air beautifully.)

[Jermey walks along the shore, his hands tucked in his pockets, head low.]

Jermey*[thinking]: What happened today... with Max. Should I propose to Rin or not?*

What if she says the same thing... that she's not ready?

After gathering so much courage to get over my fear, I decided to ask you... to propose to you. I know you won't leave me. I know it.

But the weight of my fear is so heavy... I just can't. I want to... I really want to... but....

It's not like I can't wait. I can.

But....

Ahh... I don't know.

(At my home.)

Henry*[clapping softly, impressed]* – Damn, you play guitar so well... and that song? You sing really great too.

Noah*[grinning with pride]* – Thank you so much, Ryy!

[He leans forward with a teasing smirk.] – Now, it's Rin's turn!

Me*[groaning and grabbing a cushion to hide my face]* – Mum, please tell him to shut up!

Isabelle *[laughs softly, then shrugs with a knowing look]* – Actually... she thinks she doesn't write that well. So...

Henry*[gasps dramatically, placing a hand on his chest]* – What?! Oh, come on, now I have to hear it. Please, Rinzee!

Don't make me beg!

[Everyone laughs. I roll my eyes but can't help smiling.]

I – Alright....

[Noah gazes at me and blinks.]

I –

"Why can't the pain of every single night just stop?
A night that always brings the past...
But how strange—
the darkness of night is somehow necessary.

The night becomes beautiful when we stargaze.
The moon still shines,
even when the night turns horrible.

And the stars...
they still gaze at us.
Maybe—
maybe they just want us to speak."

[A silent lingers in the room, Ryy and Mum are staring at me, while Noah sits with his head down.]

Henry *[with soft sadness, but joy in his eyes.]* – Rin... that was really, really beautiful.

Why do you think you're not good enough at writing?

Isabelle – Rin... you've absorbed an entire ocean of emotions in your heart.

[I have a tear in my eye.] – Noah...

Noah*[pressing his lips together.]* – What would I say?

Mum's right. You hold so much inside you.

Henry – Rin... you're going to have gorgeous emotional life.

I – Yeah....

CHAPTER TWENTY-FIVE

A Morning Full of Hopes

(Next morning, at school.)

Jermey – Hey Max, are you alright now?

Max – Yeah, bro. I'm totally fine.

I*[grinning, drawing out his name teasingly]* – Hi, Jer... Jer... Mey...!

Jermey *[smiling, rubbing the back of his neck slightly]* – Hey, Rinz.....!

Skye*[whispers in my ear]* – Hey, did he ask?

I – Not yet, but... I think I should!

Skye*[raising an eyebrow]* – Huh... that sounds cool! By the way, do you know what happened last night?

I*[curious, leaning in slightly]* – What...?

Skye*[whispered]* – Jace said no to Max for the Winter Formal.

[My eyes widening in surprise] – But why? He likes Max. It means Hannah was wrong?

Skye*[shaking her head]* – No... no, this time she's not.

[I'm confused] – Then?

Skye – Jace said that he's not ready to show everyone the reality of him.

[I let out a soft gasp.] – Ohh... oh...! Then, with whom will he come now?

Skye*[shrugs]* – He said he'll come alone to enjoy by himself.

I*[nodding slowly, thoughtful]* – Hmm...!

(In history class.)

[I notice Max gazing at Jace.]

I start thinking....

It's so strange how people can't show what they actually feel—even to their special ones.

But why?

Is it that they can't trust, or they feel the other person might not understand?

But.... then who will?

I think love isn't about just being with someone.

It's about seeing them happy—even when they're not with us.

What if they want the same, but it's just not happening? Should they stop loving them? Or just stop thinking about them?

But to love someone should be beautiful, right?

Then why does it hurt? Maybe to teach us that beauty includes both the good and the bad.

(At the Snowy Crumble café.)

[The afternoon sun filters through the glass, casting soft light on the table. Isabelle sits alone, her fingers wrapped around a coffee mug. She looks calm, but there's a hint of fear behind her composed expression.

The door opens—Ethan walks in.

They exchange a long look before he sits across from her.]

Isabelle*[quietly]* – I wasn't expecting you to come.

Ethan*[shrugging, avoiding eye contact]* – I wasn't sure if I should... but I came anyway.

Isabelle – I think we both know why we're here.

[*A pause. The silence isn't awkward—it's heavy.*]

Ethan – Did you tell her about Henry?

Isabelle[*nodding*] – Wow... you're asking me? She found out. From you.

Ethan[*pressing his lips together*] – I didn't mean to hurt her. I just didn't know what to do.

Isabelle – But eventually, you did. She's not a little girl anymore. She understands more than we think.

Ethan[*softly*] – I know.

Isabelle[*looking down*] – Ethan... I want peace for all of us. For her, for Noah, for myself.

Ethan[*finally meeting her eyes*] – And for you... and Henry?

Isabelle[*smiles faintly*] – Yes. For us too.

[*A long silence. Both look tired—maybe this is what peace feels like?*]

Ethan – I'll try to be better... if she lets me.

Isabelle – Ethan... give her some time. Because in the end she knows you're her dad.

And Noah knows that too.

(At the school garden.)

[*The breeze is soft, brushing against my cheeks gently.*

Jermey is standing with our friends, laughing at something Max just said. I start walking toward them.]

Ahh... I feel nervous—but there's a small spark of joy dancing in my eyes.

Because I'm about to ask Jermey.

Oh God...!

He notices me coming, his smile already forming.]

Jermey – Hey, Rinz... everything okay?

[*I nod quickly, fidgeting with my bracelet, then take a breath.*]

Me *[softly]* – Umm... I wanted to ask...

Would you go to the Winter Formal with me?

[His eyes widen just a little—then soften, his smile turning into something warm and real.]

Jermey – Rinz... yeah.

I'd love to go with Rinz... from Rinny.

[He smiles gently, like the moment means more than just a yes.]

Skye*[sighs dramatically]* – Finally...!

[Everyone laughs, and I can't help but blush a little, but inside—it feels like the happiest kind of calm.]

(When school gets over.)

Jermey*[grinning warmly]* – Come on, Rinz... I'll drop you home.

I *[nodding, smiling softly]* – Okay...!

(In the car.)

I *[looking out the window, then turning to him excitedly]* – Uh... huh... Winter Formal will be fun!

Jermey*[glancing at Rinzee with a soft smile]* – Yeah... with you, it will be.

[He taps his fingers lightly on the steering wheel, then glances at me again, eyes twinkling.]

Jermey – Then... wanna go to Giana beach now?

[I blink in surprise, then my face lights up.] – Yeah.... Let's go!

(At the beach.)

[Jermey and I walk side by side, the cool breeze brushing against us.]

[Suddenly, Jermey scoops up some water droplets and splashes them onto my face before darting away, laughing.]

[I gasp, eyes widening, then break into a grin.] – Jermey...!

[*We start running along the edge of the waves, laughter mixing with the sound of the ocean.*]

[**Jermey glances back at Rinzee, his eyes softening.**] – I've never seen someone's face so light up like that... your eyes become so cute when you smile.

[**I feel my cheeks turn even warmer. I look down shyly for a second, then meet his eyes, smiling behind my hand.**] – Yeah... with you, I can't stop smiling. [*I giggle, covering my mouth.*]

The Night We've Been Waiting For

(At my home.)

Isabelle – Rin, which dress were you supposed to wear tonight?

[I sighed.] – Yeah... I think...

Henry – Don't think—when I'm here.

[I blinked, a little surprised as he stepped in, holding something behind his back.]

Henry*[with a soft smile.]* – Rinz... I got you a new dress. Your favourite colour—blue.

[I bounce in excitement.] – Wow... Eeee....! Thank you so much, Ryy!

Isabelle*[watched us, a spark of joy in her eyes, thinking]*: May my kiddos... get all happiness they truly deserve.

Henry – Where's Noah? I brought a formal for him too.

Isabelle – He's in his room.

(In Noah's room.)

Henry – Hey, Noah!

Noah – Oh... hey, Ryy!

Henry – Look, Noah — I got you a new outfit too!

Henry holds out a sleek black blazer, paired with a crisp white shirt and neatly pressed black trousers.)

Noah *[grinning]* – Black, huh? Nice... you know my style!

Henry *[laughs]* – Gotta make sure you look sharp tonight.

[Noah takes the outfit, tossing it casually over his shoulder.]

Noah – Thanks, Ryy. Guess I'll be turning a few heads tonight too.

(Noah and I get ready and come downstairs to leave for the Winter Formal.)

Isabelle*[beaming]* – Aww... you both look so adorable!

Henry [grinning] – Yeah.... Really!

[Noah and I smile softly.]

Both – Thank you so much!

(At the Winter Formal.)

[The beach glows under the soft fairy lights, as if the stars have come a little closer and are twinkling just above us. Little by little, soft flakes of snow fall gently over the beach, stopping and starting, like the sky itself is feeling love—taking deep, quiet breaths. The cool breeze carries the salty scent of the ocean.]

[I clutch Noah's arm a little tighter, both excited and nervous.]

Noah*[whispering]* – This is unreal... snow at the beach?

I *[smiling]* – I know... it's like a magic. This is the beauty of Georgiana — a blanket of snow at the beach.

Giana is the most beautiful beach in this city.

(We walk slowly across the soft, cold sand, hearing laughter and music blending with the sound of the waves.

I spot Skye and Cyrus among the crowd.)

Skye*[grinning]* – Look who's here! Rin... you're looking really pretty.

I*[smile warmly]* – Aww... Thank you! You too.

Noah*[smirking]* – Someone found someone... so now they've stopped noticing the rest!

Skye*[dramatically]* – No... it's not like that! You look so handsome too!

(Daisy spots Noah.)
Daisy[*smiling brightly*] – Hey, baby!
Noah[*takes a deep breath, grinning, gazing into her eyes*] – Oh baby... you look so beautiful, like a daisy flower.
[Noah steps even closer to her.]
Noah [*whispers*] – Can I...?
Daisy[*blushing warmly*] – Yes, you can.
[They kiss, the snowfall softly wrapping around them like a blessing.]
Skye[*teasingly*] – Now someone's got someone too...
[Noah laughs, rolling his eyes and shrugging]
[Daisy's cheeks turn warm with a blush.]
[I look around, searching for Jermey.] – Where's everyone else?
Cyrus – Don't know!
(On the other side of the beach.)
(Max notices Jermey standing alone, gazing at the waves, lost in thoughts.)
Max – Hey, Jermey... what happened, bro? Why are you standing here all alone?
Jermey[*pressing his lips together*] – I thought of proposing to Rinz...
Max – Wow... man! Then what are you waiting for? Just do it. We're all eagerly waiting for this moment.
Jermey[*head down, drawing something with his toe in the sand*] – But... my fear.... You know how heavy it feels on my shoulders.
Max – Jermey...
Jermey – And she's already going through so much. How can someone like me...
Max[*putting a hand on his shoulder*] – Jermey, don't overthink. Just give it a chance.

Otherwise, you'll regret it your whole life for not even trying.

Jermey – But...

Max – Sometimes, we make our inner battles so violent, that we don't even notice they were always silent.

So just give it a try. You already know... she's the one.

Cyrus – Look there, Hannah is enjoying her own company, dancing with herself.

Skye – It took so much courage to do that, you know!

Cyrus – I know... and only Hannah can do this.

[He shouts, grinning] – Go, girl, Hannah!

[Hannah grins and waves at them, making her way back toward the group.]

Skye*[softly, with admiration]* – But this time... Max too!

[Nearby, I step a little away from the crowd, wrapping my arms around myself, breathing in the cool, salty air.

The soft snowfall kisses my hair and cheeks. Smiling quietly, I cup my palms over my cheeks, feeling their warmth against the winter chill. I close my eyes for a second, swaying gently to the faint music playing far behind — feeling at peace, just me, the waves, the snow, and the stars.]

[Jermey is standing few steps away, gazing at Rinzee.]

Jermey*[thinking]: Oh... God! How beautiful she looks. Aww... a blue dress, the beach and the snowfall.*

I wonder... is this what a dream proposal looks like?

Jermey, don't lose this chance.

[He looks at the moon.]

"What do you say?"

Moon – *"Just go, man. Ask your star to vanish your scars."*

[Jermey smiles.]

(Jermey moves toward Rinzee.)

Jermey*[takes a deep breath]* – Rinz...

[I grin.] – Where were you? I was looking for you.

Jermey *[in a shaky voice]* – I….

[I stare into his eyes.] – Mmm… someone is looking so handsome today!

Jermey*[blushes, his nervousness peeking through.]* – Rinz… I want to say something to you…

[I tilt my head slightly, curiosity blooming inside me.]

Jermey*[voice trembling slightly]* – Rinz… I don't know how to say it perfectly… but I'll try.

[He takes a step closer, looking straight into her eyes.]

[The soft flakes of snow kiss my cheeks, and the sound of the waves makes everything feel even more dreamy.]

Jermey –

"Somewhere between the chaos and understanding,
the beautiful star twinkles—that is love.
The blink of your eyes made me think
to always remain in your sight.
The initial of your context
reminds me of every single eye contact.
The entry of you in my life
feels like… maybe I should retry.
The way you speak—
every time, I become more freak.
Somewhere behind the oceans,
there is a place where I imagine us.
Like, listen to my quiet voice—
behind in my mind, it just says,
"I'm waiting for you."
Like, listen and understand
the lyrics of my heart,
behind my blood, by heart.
Somewhere between two hearts,
there is a thread connecting them.
And I want this rare star

to always shine...
and twinkle love for me."
[My eyes widen. I put my hand over my mouth, grinning, my cheeks warmed with blush.]
I – *Jermey... I... I don't even have words.*
[My eyes glisten slightly as I laugh quietly.]
[My voice trembles, but I step closer.]
I – *I can't believe that after everything that happened these past months, someone could still say so much... and feel so much for me.*
I never imagined a proposal this dreamy....
Even I want you too in my life.
Because someday, just hearing about you — without even knowing you — I still felt something.
And the thought of you lit my soul, and the blink of your eyes made my heart twinkle.
[He smiles, and I smile back, feeling the whole world disappear around us — just him and me, under the snowy sky and the fairy lights twinkling in our hearts.]
[Jermey and I kiss, gazing into each other's eyes.]
[We enter the crowd, holding hands, where everyone is dancing.]
[Everyone looks at us, smiling and whispers – "Wow... finally... Aww..."]
Skye*[excitedly]* – Rin....! *[showing the sparkle of joy in her eyes.]*
[I grin and nod my head.]
Max*[smiling, nodding his head]* – Jermey... man...
[Jermey blushes.]
Cyrus and Hannah*[grinning and staring.]*
[Jermey and I exchange a glance.]
Noah*[jumping excitedly, pumping his fist in the air]* – Wait... Wait.... Wait.... Yay....! This is what I was eagerly

waiting for!

Daisy[*giggling, playfully nudging Noah's arm.*] – Georgiana is lucky for girls.

Jermey [smirking, glancing at me] – Not only for girls.

[*I laugh softly, squeezing his hand a little tighter.*]

I[*pressing my lips together, smiling*] – Maybe we both wanted that too.

[*We start dancing, staring into each other's eyes.*]

I start thinking....

Mum.... she was right. Maybe a new place could bring joy into our lives.

Our family feels complete here.

Noah and I found love, found friends.

Within a year, my life turned into magic...

From the Rinzee who had started losing trust in love after losing his father, Joe...

Now, I have someone who love me so much...

Someone who will remember the lyrics of my heart — by heart.

Jermey[*softly whispers*] – What happened?

[*I nod my head.*] – Nothing...

(After some time, Jermey and I are walking along the beach.)

Jermey – I love you, Rinz...

I [*blushing*] – I love you too, Jer... Jer... Mey...!

Jermey[*sighing and grinning*] – You know, I already had the moon... and now, I have a star too, which...

[*I kiss his cheek.*] – Which will always make your heart twinkle.

Jermey [*blushing,* kisses on her forehead too.] -Yeah...!

I'm thinking...

Maybe every girl will find their love like this....

What if we gone through the pain, things hurt very hard....

But.... but... but... you never know what Miracle is waiting for you...!